A Candlelight Ecstasy Romance

"KISS ME," SHE WHISPERED, BARELY ABLE TO BREATHE . . . .

She smiled at the naked need in his beautiful, sensuous eyes. She had bargained for a kiss, but she got much more than that. Fiercely he pinned her to him with one arm, and with his free hand clutched her open blouse at the back of the neck and wrenched it down, trapping her arms behind her within its folds. Twisting so that she was now pressed hard beneath him, he finally took her mouth and kissed it violently. And he kept demanding her mouth, again and again . . . .

LOVE'S WINE

Frances Flores

A CANDLELIGHT ECSTASY ROMANCE™

Publishing by
Dell Publishing Co., Inc.
1 Dag Hammarskjold Plaza
New York, New York 10017

Copyright © 1982 by Frances de Talavera Berger

All rights reserved. No part of this book may be
reproduced or transmitted in any form or by any
means, electronic or mechanical, including photocopying,
recording, or by any information storage
and retrieval system, without the written permission
of the Publisher, except where permitted by law.

Dell ® TM 681510, Dell Publishing Co., Inc.

Candlelight Ecstasy Romance™ is a trademark of
Dell Publishing Co., Inc., New York, New York.

ISBN: 0-440-14785-9

Printed in the United States of America
First printing—June 1982

Dear Reader:

In response to your continued enthusiasm for Candlelight Ecstasy Romances™, we are increasing the number of new titles from four to six per month.

We are delighted to present sensuous novels set in America, depicting modern American men and women as they confront the provocative problems of modern relationships.

Throughout the history of the Candlelight line, Dell has tried to maintain a high standard of excellence, to give you the finest in reading enjoyment. That is now and will remain our most ardent ambition.

Anne Gisonny
Editor
Candlelight Romances

LOVE'S WINE

CHAPTER ONE

Vic Remo was having a hard time believing his eyes. He had driven all the way out to the center of the Valley of the Moon to haggle with an old woman named Laura D'Asti Spandoni, and he had just received quite a shock.

Laura didn't squirm under the pressure of his stare. Instead, she went right on with her work, remaining on her knees on the warm, fruitful earth. Her hands never stopped exploring the texture of each tender leaf.

"You're Mrs. Spandoni? I don't believe it!"

A little annoyed, Laura finally glanced up at the intruder. The hot sun was high in the midday sky, and she couldn't see him too well. "Mr. Remo, I'm sorry, but I'm sure you can see I'm very busy." There was so much work to be done here in the vineyards. There was also so little time, so little money, and so little help! "Exactly what is it you want?"

"It's not a question of what I want. It's a question of what you may want, Mrs. Spandoni."

The beguiling statement plus the unmistakable trace of implied forcefulness in his voice provoked Laura into twisting around to face this man. She lifted her arm slowly, using her tapered fingers to shield her eyes from the sun's glare. This casual, natural movement seemed to incite a slight difference in Vic Remo's breathing pattern. This amused Laura, but she chose to ignore it. What she couldn't ignore any longer, however, was the fact that this confrontation between herself and the unknown Mr. Remo was becoming somewhat silly. Even more ridiculous, her brief cutoffs and flimsy shirt were beginning to cling tightly to her moist skin, leaving exposed much more than the bare lengths of her bronzed arms and legs. But it wasn't Laura's nature to be flustered for long. Quickly dusting away specks of earth from her palms and thighs, she rose to her feet. "I prefer to be called Laura D'Asti again—I'm not Mrs. Spandoni anymore—and to be perfectly honest, all I want at this moment is to be left alone to finish my work. I don't mean to be rude, but owning and operating this Winery doesn't leave me too much time for philosophical small talk. . . ."

She had meant to be blunt, but the impact of her rebuke was spoiled. The words abruptly died in her throat. For the first time she really saw Vic Remo. He was standing a good distance away and the sunny glare still bedeviled her sight, but suddenly every physical detail of the man etched itself in her mind as deeply as if he had loomed whisperingly close to her. His was the kind of face that attracted by its very paradoxes. Strong, almost hard, it was a face that was saved from slipping into brutality by the way the blue-black hair softly curved along his head to the base of his neck, by the shimmer that shot out from his raven eyes, but mostly by the betraying fullness of his sensitive, sensual mouth. He didn't tower over Laura, yet he dominated every inch of space around him. Now he shifted his body ever so slightly, revealing just a hint of temper. Laura liked that; she was glad she hadn't intimidated him. Still, he had shaken her self-assurance, so she quickly continued. "What I mean is, who are you, Mr. Remo?" She gazed carefully at the well-worn but obviously very expensive cord pants and jacket and hand-tooled boots he was wearing. "Why have you come all the way from San Francisco to see me?"

"I'm a wine broker," he answered, then smiled for the first time. It was a wonderful smile. "And you've guessed correctly, I am from San Francisco. Is that why you've taken an instant dislike to me—Signorina D'Asti?"

"You've been reading too many bad novels." Laura laughed in spite of herself. "We *rustici* out here in Napa-Sonoma no longer tremble at the sight of a sophisticated stranger from *la città* twirling his mustache, you know." She swept her long auburn hair atop her head with a lovely carelessness that would have been devastating if she had meant it to be, but she was merely freeing her small neck and shoulders from its heavy, luxuriant burden. "No, I don't dislike you, Mr. Remo, for the simple reason that I don't know you. You say you're a wine broker. What are you selling?"

Thoughtfulness all but erased Vic's smile. "I'm buying, not selling."

"Oh, well, then." She really laughed, letting her hair go free and shaking it loose. It floated around her face like dark-gold foam. "I'm afraid we're both wasting our time."

"Are you sure?"

"Of course! Look, I assume you're a very successful wine broker—"

"You might call me that."

"And I'm sure you have a great deal of expertise in the wine business, don't you?"

"I have."

"Then surely you must know that my family has never sold our wine through outside agents! We're small but exclusive, and right from the beginning we've always produced the best wines in California. The D'Asti label and the D'Asti reputation are all we've ever needed to ensure a complete sellout of our vintage stock." She willed herself to speak the next words with as much strength and conviction as she could muster, although a hollow fear haunted her waking hours and sleepless nights. "I inherited this great Winery from my father, and he inherited it from his father. My great-grandfather brought over the original vine cuttings from the vineyards in northern Italy that he had inherited from *his* father. I intend to carry on the D'Asti tradition in every way, believe me, Mr. Remo." She took a deep breath and flung back her head. "I don't intend to change any of our methods of growing, harvesting, or marketing, so . . ."

"I didn't come here to buy the D'Asti wine."

Laura was genuinely startled. Vic Remo hadn't moved a muscle, nor had he come a step closer, but he suddenly seemed to have reached out and touched her coldly. Without quite knowing why, Laura immediately felt threatened. "I don't understand. If not the wines, then what did you come to buy?"

"Laura . . . Miss D'Asti, couldn't we go somewhere else to talk?"

That same note of forcefulness in his voice reappeared. Laura sensed that if she gave in to his plea she would be unleashing something irretrievable, perhaps even destructive. But her inquisitive, intelligent nature motivated her to find out what was at the bottom of this mystery. Besides, Vic Remo intrigued her. No, honest with herself as always, she admitted she was more than merely intrigued. He radiated a quality of inner strength, all the more fascinating because it was a commodity she had never yet encountered in a man. "Is it really important? Tell me the truth."

"It's very important—for you. Trust me."

That seemed to cinch it for Laura. "All right."

A cry from the field jabbed at Laura's nerves like the stab of a needle. "Lauretta! Lauretta! *Ciao, padrona, ciao!*" A smiling fieldworker, his gnarled, ancient hands waggling a signal for Laura to follow him, popped out from the middle of a cluster of vines. "*Abbiamo gìa fatti la prova del terreno. Tutté bene!* Come and take a look, Lauretta."

"*Gioia, Beppo!* I'm so happy! I'll be right there."

The venerable employee nodded, turned away, but then hesitated. His eyes, twinkling and full of fondness, flicked from Laura to Vic. A second later he disappeared as swiftly as he had appeared, but only after he had expressed himself most eloquently with an exaggerated Romanesque shrug.

"Protective old coot, isn't he?" Vic said, not unkindly. He strolled closer to Laura, and that warm smile was very much in evidence again. "Who is he, a relative?"

She shook her lovely head. "Beppo is practically a fixture here in the Valley of the Moon. He's my foreman in the fields. Legend has it that he planted the very first grapes in Napa-Sonoma!" Laura looked Vic Remo over frankly now that he had ventured closer to her. It surprised her to see the few highly engaging wisps of silver along the temples. How old was he? she wondered. Forty, perhaps, forty-one? Whichever, damn, he was handsome! Giving in to an involuntary, thoroughly feminine impulse, she peeked at his left hand to see if he wore a wedding band. But his hands were casually resting in his jacket pockets, and she couldn't tell. Now what on earth had made her wonder about such a stupid detail? To compensate for her momentary foolishness, she returned to the innocuous subject of old Beppo. "No, Beppo's not a relative, but I love him dearly. It's also true he's become overly protective since Frank Spandoni died."

Laura had guessed correctly when she had assumed Vic Remo was a successful businessman: his urbane manner, his expensive clothes, and the elegent European sports car parked alongside the dirt road all pointed to that fact. What she couldn't have guessed was that he had risen to the top of a very competitive field by noticing and remembering every nuance, every detail in even the most nonchalant conversation. Now he had been impressed by the way Laura's voice had warmed when she had spoken about Beppo, an old D'Asti farmhand, yet had shown no emotion whatsoever when she had mentioned Frank Spandoni. Vic had done his homework, and he knew that Frank Spandoni had been in his mid-sixties when he had been killed in an accident. This unbelievably stunning woman was young. But in spite of the tremendous difference in their ages, Laura *had* been Frank Spandoni's wife, hadn't she? What was bothering the hell out of Vic now was that he had been able to learn very little about the widowed Mrs. Spandoni. He had naturally assumed she was an elderly woman. Boy, had he been wrong! Being wrong was a weakness Vic Remo didn't allow himself too often. He had been silently castigating himself for that one mistake from the moment he had driven up to the field and had first caught sight of Laura D'Asti. Although he was still sparring with his badly bruised ego, he managed to appear calm. "Well, anyway, I'm happy for your sake and for Beppo's, too, that the soil tests turned out so well. Tricky thing, keeping the soil balanced just right, isn't it? It can make or break a crop. But then, the D'Asti vineyards have been famous for a hundred years for their 'noble' soil, haven't they." It was a statement, not a question.

Laura blinked in surprise. "You understood what Beppo said! Funny, I didn't think you knew Italian."

"If you knew me—which you don't, remember—you'd find out I'm full of surprises."

Beppo's strident call again pierced the silence. "Lauretta!"

"I'd better go," she said, looking over her shoulder and returning her gaze to Vic Remo. What was there about him that was so tantalizing, so evasive? "If you don't mind waiting, we can meet at my house. We can talk there without being interrupted, all right?"

"Sounds fine to me."

"Actually, I'll probably get there before you do. If you just follow this side road back along the edge of the vineyard, you'll bump right into the main road and that will take you through our gates and right up to our house. You can't miss it. The house itself is a large white Victorian relic—"

"I know. I pulled up to the house looking for you. A very elderly lady told me where I could find you." He didn't add that he had immediately mistaken the old crone for the widow Spandoni!

"That must have been Donna Evangelina," Laura said

with just the correct touch of respect in her voice. "She's my mother-in-law." Vic received a smile that began hesitantly, then grew to brilliance. "See you in a few minutes." Laura left, running swiftly between the vines.

"You damned, stupid, asinine fool!" Vic cursed himself softly but soundly. He stood there, staring into the void where Laura had been only a moment before, grinding the heel of his boot into the soil as if he had suddenly developed a personal grudge against it. When he finally climbed into his car, he slammed the door shut behind him with a loud bang, gunned the motor unmercifully, and spun out onto the dirt road, leaving clouds of dust rising for yards into the air.

Twenty minutes later, when he hit the main road, he almost laughed remembering how different his mood had been as he drove along the same stretch earlier that morning. Then Vic Remo had owned the world. He had left San Francisco in a relaxed mood, absolutely sure of himself, knowing everything he touched would turn to gold. He had felt no need to hurry or worry. He was only mildly challenged by his assignment—to buy the D'Asti Winery. Actually he was heading out to Napa-Sonoma to buy much more than just a famous old winery; it was the D'Asti integrity and reputation he was intent on purchasing, too. The simple business transaction would pose no great problem because although the D'Asti family had continued somehow to produce superb wines, the whole operation was coming apart at the seams, very nearly bankrupt. Worse, the Winery had been left in the shaky hands of Frank Spandoni's old widow!

Vic had been so sure of his easy success that he had decided to make it a fun day and had deliberately taken the long way to Sonoma. The Golden Gate Bridge had looked gorgeous, and he took the time to notice the fleet of puffy white sails on the bay, each catching just enough of the wind to glide gaily along the sparkling blue water. What a jolt those early adventuring Spaniards must have experienced when, the fog finally lifting away from the narrow straits at its mouth, they saw this magnificent bay for the first time! Now hundreds of feet above it, Vic had smiled at the crowds of strollers, joggers, dogs, bicycles, and lovers crisscrossing the length of the bridge.

He had left the bridge itself just where the road spiraled down to the quaint town of Sausalito, once the "Little Willow" of the old settlers but now a thriving Mecca for tourists. Ahead had loomed the colorful, rainbow-painted tunnel entrance to Marin County, and then he had merged into the main stream of the freeway, which took him due north past Mount Tamalpais, the mountain of the Sleeping Princess, with her hands seemingly covering her misty breasts. Even the usually disturbing sight of Frank Lloyd Wright's Marin Civic Center had not blighted Vic's mood. Squatting and malevolent, this strange building, anchored forever to the Marin Hills, had always reminded him of some giant interplanetary bug!

In a short time, he had turned right off the freeway and onto the Black Point bypass, where he had driven along the edges of the marshes and the flats of drying salt beds. The vivid whiteness of the land reflected the rays of the sun and blinded him momentarily. The highway then narrowed to a two-lane road, and flocks of sea gulls had escorted his futuristic sports car into a world of yesteryear. Near Jack London's ill-starred Wolf House undulating pastures rose to nourish the thousands of miles of green vines that were the bearers of grapes whose fame had become international. He was in Napa-Sonoma's heartland—blessed, cherished, christened, and still called by the haunting name bestowed upon it by the early Californianos, the Valley of the Moon.

Vic now retraced his earlier drive to the D'Asti property outside Sonoma in a very different state of mind from this morning's euphoria. He was angry, and he knew damned well why: Laura D'Asti. Canova should have warned him. Vic was positive Canova had known all about the Winery's new boss lady; Canova made it his business to know such facts. That was why Vic had agreed to act as his agent in some mutually lucrative deals; he and Canova both handled their business lives and their personal lives the same way—meticulously, unemotionally, and ruthlessly.

When he approached the D'Asti gates again, Vic was beginning to regain his self-control. He realized he had attacked this assignment the wrong way. He had been thrown for a loop by the real Laura Spandoni, or Laura D'Asti, as she preferred to call herself, and he'd better change his tactics. He drove quickly past the old oak casks used as signs, beautifully preserved and freshly painted. Now he could allow himself a laugh. It was all a fake. The lovingly kept lane, bordered on each side by high poplar trees and rough-hewn wooden fences, cut right through the lush, manicured vineyards. The sight was overwhelming.

Vic brought the car to a stop alongside an arbor that was covered with a riot of colorful wisteria. He swiftly walked around the romantic hedge and onto a lawn as soft and downy as a cushion. Before him stood the proud D'Asti mansion, complete with its fantastic Victorian gingerbread embellishments, its classic three-story white frame, its gables, its widow's walk, and its peaked roofs.

How many times had he picked up a bottle of premium D'Asti wine and admired the tasteful reproduction of this house on the label? Now he was seeing the mansion as he had never seen it before; Laura D'Asti had just come through the front door. The sight of her framed by the graceful doorway was almost breathtaking. But he knew her secret: Everything about this place was a deliberate, calculated illusion!

"Hello! What took you so long? Come on up here, and we can sit on the steps and talk."

Vic strolled halfway up the staircase and sat down a step or two below Laura. She had found the time to change clothes, and he silently saluted her swift actions. Most women he knew would have purposely kept him waiting. Also, most women he knew would have looked dowdy in the clothes she had chosen—jeans, denim shirt, espadrilles, and a matching blue scarf tightly wound around her head and knotted severely at the back of her neck. But she managed somehow to look childlike and vulnerable. Oh, she was beautiful, all right, but Vic wasn't fooled. She was also smart as hell.

"Ah, Bella! Where have you been, honey?" The strangest-looking dog Vic had ever seen came paddling out of the house and quickly plopped itself down next to Laura. The animal, squat, sturdy, and built long and low like a dachshund, had great tufts of long, rusty-red hair sprouting out of its hide. *Pretty* was not a word that came easily to mind when viewing this unusual creature, but it maintained its dignity in spite of its incongruous name. It surveyed Vic with a steady, clear warning in its eye. But Bella was also capable of worship; a juicy lick at Laura's elbow proved that.

"I would venture the opinion that that's not your ordinary household-variety dog," Vic said, leaning back on the next step, a smile hovering around his lips.

"Oh, no, Bella's quite unique. Hers is a traditional breed in Italy, but you won't find too many like her in California. But don't let her unusual appearance fool you," she warned, neither petting nor fussing over the dog yet conveying a deep love, "because she's actually a ferocious hunter."

"Oh, I'm ready to take your word for it!"

A beat or two of silence passed and then she said evenly, "All right, Mr. Remo, let's get down to business. What is it you want to buy from me?"

"The Winery."

"My Winery's not for sale."

"You know, I find that hard to believe." He was direct and candid. "If I owned this Winery and had the financial problems you have, I would have sold out long ago."

She sat very still and looked straight at Vic, her eyes wide and clear. "Long ago? I don't understand. I think you're under some mistaken impression. . . ."

"I'm afraid you're the one who has made the mistake, Laura. This whole operation should have been sold at least two years ago when your husband died."

"Why?"

"I told you, I'm a wine broker. But I also specialize in vineyard production, marketing, and sales. I've made a study of the D'Asti Winery's financial record, and my honest advice to you is sell, cut your losses, and salvage as much money as you can."

"But I don't recall asking your advice, Mr. Remo." She was jarred, but she didn't stoop to easy hysterics. "Who gave you permission to stick your nose into my finances?" This time there was steel under the velvet voice.

"I don't need your permission. Laura, please listen to me. Business audits are a matter of public record, and these audits are required reading in my profession. But I didn't even have to go that deeply into the records. I knew you were involved in a tragic financial mess merely by talking to your suppliers, who haven't been paid. Your field hands haven't been paid, either."

"Is that also a required tactic in your profession, sneaking around talking to my fieldworkers?"

"Just a minute." His male ego asserted itself. "I use my intelligence and my experience and anything else that's legal to get what I want. I gather information from all sources, and I don't consider that 'sneaking around,' as you so bluntly put it. But if you want to be blunt, then I'll be blunt, too. You're bankrupt. You know it and I know it. Almost everybody in this valley knows it." He stood up suddenly, took a few steps down, and then turned to face Laura again. He was about to use his most potent argument, but he felt slightly rotten about doing it. Why? He was telling her the truth, wasn't he? "Be realistic. It's obvious you love this place very much. I don't think you could bear to just stand by and watch your family's name and reputation go down the drain. But if you continue operating at a loss, that's exactly what's going to happen because I know you haven't enough money to keep this business alive for another month. You're about to lose everything. If you act right now, you can still save the Winery's prestige and also wind up with a great deal of money for yourself. Don't you understand? You have no choice but to sell out. Won't you even consider it?"

"No." Although she said it quietly, it carried the impact of a fervent vow.

"Everything I've been telling you is true. . . ."

"No!"

"Do you realize how much money is involved? You'd be rich. . . ."

"*No!*" This time a shudder passed through her body. Shifting a little closer to her mistress, Bella lifted her snout and sniffed the air, her instincts aroused by the smell of danger.

"Then I'm sorry, believe me." Vic knew he had applied enough pressure for the time being. The next time he presented Laura D'Asti with the same proposition things would go more smoothly, the pendulum would swing in his favor. A difficult element to bend, pride; he knew from his own experience. He slowly remounted the steps until he was almost eye level with Laura. "Here's my business card, anyway. If you change your mind, won't you please call me?" He placed the white embossed card on the step next to her, deliberately just out of arm's reach.

"Mr. Remo?"

Almost across the lawn, he stopped but didn't turn around. He had thought this beautiful young woman would put up more of a fight, show a little more spunk. Shrugging off his slight disappointment, he faced her again. "Yes, Miss D'Asti?"

She was still sitting on the step, and she moved only to wrap her arms around her knees, hugging herself closer. The business card remained untouched. "You've asked me to face the truth. How would you react, I wonder, if I asked you to face a miracle?"

"Well," he thought, "at least her approach is refreshingly offbeat, anyway!" "Is that a rhetorical question, or do you really expect an answer?"

"I'm quite serious."

Intrigued, he carefully kept the conversation going. "I

don't know how I would react. I've never encountered a miracle in my line of work."

"Perhaps the experience might change your attitude. Maybe you've become too cynical, too practical." One easy, fluid move carried her forward to stand on her feet. "Well, are you game?"

"How can I resist such a challenge?"

"I somehow guessed you were the kind of man who couldn't resist a challenge." She came down the stairs, Bella bounding along behind her. "Just follow me. And don't worry, I'm not crazy." The irony of her next words hit Vic squarely. "Trust me!"

The homey, old-fashioned qualities of the property were evident the minute Laura led Vic away from the grandeur of the mansion. Ordinary farm equipment dating back to the twenties stood about like rusty relics. Weathered, unpainted wooden workhouses appeared all over the landscape in a haphazard fashion, and the air echoed with the raucous noises of various domestic animals. Everything looked seedy and slightly neglected. Off the main path, someone had planted an impressive garden of iris, quince, lavender, and hedge roses. The scent from this array was enough to seduce the senses, but Vic seemed to be more interested in the vegetables growing in well-tended rows within the border of flowers.

"I thought you were only interested in grapes," Laura murmured.

"Now, yes, but I grew up learning everything there is to know about these," he said, pointing to the choice *carciofi, zucchini, cicòri, pomadòri,* and *broccolirappen* sprouting from the ground. The missionaries had charted the first farms in the Valley of the Moon under Spanish grants, but the area bloomed today through the backbreaking efforts of the immigrant Italian farmers who found much to their joy that traditional Italian vegetables flourished in this new-world soil.

"Was your father a farmer?" She couldn't hide her surprise.

"No." He laughed, but with little mirth. "My parents owned a very small vegetable store in San Francisco." He bent and picked one of the fat pear-shaped *pomadòri* and bit into it. "Great! I'd call this a miracle, wouldn't you? Is this your garden?"

"No. It's my mother-in-law's garden. She spends a great deal of time on it since she has very little else to do. Shall we go on?"

Keeping his thoughts to himself, Vic finished the tomato as Laura quickly led him toward an interlocked group of buildings beautifully covered with masses of pale wisteria creepers. "These are the original buildings," she said, rubbing her palms gently against the old stone walls, "so please be very, very careful and watch your step inside. The floors are very uneven and dangerous."

"This is the famous tasting room, isn't it?" he said, entering a cool, damp room that glowed from the late-afternoon light coming through a solitary window. He recognized the elaborately carved walls and the massive mahogany bar. "I've seen it many times in historic photographs."

"Yes, but I closed it to the public two years ago. I try to keep it clean and polished, but it still gets a little musty in here," she apologized, showing a strange nervousness for the first time. She hurried over to a small side door and thrust it open. "Ah, that's better." Bella, who had been following underfoot all the way, carried out a weird, rapid pattern of sniffs mixed with barks, and then shot through the door like a flash.

"Why? I mean, why did you close down this room?"

Laura's answer was drowned out completely by a hideous, shrill screech coming from somewhere beyond the small door. Neither of them moved for a second. Then Vic bolted for the door with Laura right behind him. "No, Bella! Stop it!"

The source of the mayhem was easy to spot. A stately corps of red-billed geese had been in the process of striding across a tiny bridge spanning a pond when disaster had struck. Bella, succumbing to some primeval urge deep within her, still had her fangs in the hind quarters of the unfortunate goose that happened to be last in the parade. Amid a storm of feathers, growls, flapping wings, and squalls, with Laura pulling at the goose and Vic putting pressure on Bella's snout, peace and order was finally restored. "You march right back to the house!" Laura commanded, snapping her fingers sharply in front of the dog's nose. "Go!" Bella, sadly penitent, immediately obeyed. "I'm sorry," Laura sighed, relieved to see the goose, more injured in dignity than in body, take quickly to the water. "Bella's usually beautifully behaved around the farm animals. I don't know what got into her today! Still, I hate to punish her for doing something that is natural to her instincts."

"You're right. It never works when you fight nature, does it?" If Vic was conscious of the streak of mockery that ran through his words, he didn't show it. His smile was light, and he looked Laura straight in the eye while absentmindedly brushing away some feathers from his jacket sleeve.

"What happened to your hand? Oh, God, Bella bit you!"

Surprised, Vic glanced down at his hand. "It's nothing. Forget it."

"That's not true! It's a deep, ugly wound, and it's bleeding. There's a first-aid kit in the cellars. Hurry!"

The path to the cellars took them back through the tasting room and down a steep flight of stairs. This was the very heart of the Winery. Here, the wine was fermented, aged, allowed to rest, and finally bottled. While Laura hastily searched for the first-aid kit, Vic took the opportunity to study the layout. The only modern equipment he could see were the many stainless-steel fermenting vats. Everything else, from the magnificent oak aging casks, which were individually inscribed with the names of Italian patron saints, to the ceiling-high bottle repositories, was superbly old-world and absurdly time-consuming and costly in this day and age.

"Ah, I found it," Laura said, holding the first-aid kit aloft triumphantly. "Now, let's go over to that table—oh, Matt! I didn't know you were down here."

A big, curiously boyish-looking man had wound his way around the huge casks and walked toward Laura. He had sandy hair that matched sandy eyes and glasses. Midthirties and shy as a twelve-year-old—that described him, although to some women he might appear quite attractive. "Did you forget? I told you last night I thought it was time to rack and check the bentonite balance in this row of casks. I wish you would listen to me, Laura. I can't keep this premium asleep much longer. . . ."

"Matt! We've already discussed that, and I don't want to talk about it now," she interrupted rather sharply, aware Vic was showing a keen interest in the conversation.

"Sure, Laura, whatever you say." He shrugged in resignation and then glanced at Vic.

"Mr. Remo, this is Matt Moyer, my lab expert." Laura tried to smooth away her temper of a moment ago. "Matt's the real genius who has kept our wine first-rate." The two men sized each other up silently and nodded their hellos. If Matt wondered who Mr. Remo might be, he kept the question to himself. Laura seemed to have a sudden inspiration. "I'm sure Beppo's looking for you. He's finished taking the soil tests. Why don't you go and find him, Matt?"

"Yes, I'll do that." He began to say something else, then changed his mind. With another curt nod to Vic, he left.

It was obvious Laura dismissed Matt Moyer from her thoughts the minute he left the cellars. "Let's see that hand now, Mr. Remo."

A pensive smile curled around the corners of Vic's full lips. "Don't you think you could unbend a little and call me Vic? I like calling you Laura, but it's damned awkward if you keep insisting on calling me Mr. Remo."

"All right. Now give me your hand, Vic."

He extended his lacerated left hand and laid it in her palm. Bella's teeth had entered the flesh on the outside of the dark, muscular hand just below the wristbone, and the glint of gold there momentarily caught Laura's eye. Vic wore a very slim watch attached to a beautiful strap of solid beaten gold. A name or word was engraved on the surface of the precious metal, but she couldn't read it in the dim light. What she did notice immediately was that there was no wedding band on the third finger. Of course not! If she had assessed Vic Remo's character correctly, marriage was a deadly trap he would never suffer. She stifled the slight tremor that coursed through her own fingers and concentrated on applying a very neat bandage with a maximum of skill and a minimum of further damage to her own composure. Damaged. Yes, that's how she felt at this moment. She had been struggling futilely all afternoon to keep her intensifying emotions suppressed. She had felt with panic her resolve sweep away; feeling nothing at all had almost become a habit. Now this man had penetrated her safe world and easily ripped it apart. It hadn't been his astute knowledge of the Winery's money problems that had hurt so much, either. Now that she thought about it, Matt Moyer certainly knew the truth, her sister, Tina, was beginning to grow suspicious, and it was possibly true that the whole matter was an open secret in the industry. No, that part hadn't really hurt because she was holding an ace that she was sure would save the Winery. What had really hurt so desperately was the systematic, experienced way he had torn down her emotional defenses, one by one, from the instant she had gazed into those audacious, arrogant eyes. Oh, he was so controlled, so sure of himself! She suspected he had the kind of male vanity that fed on the constant adoration of women. She was also positive he had no trouble at all snagging willing victims. Well, that was his business, not hers. Let him feed his ego at somebody else's expense, Laura decided. She wasn't about to let herself be burned! "I'm finished. However, I think you should have a doctor look at your hand tomorrow."

"I don't think so." He flexed the hand. "It feels fine. Thanks. Now, let's forget about this and change the subject. Have you forgotten you promised me a miracle?"

"I remember. First, let me show you something." She walked to the darkest part of the cellars where a wine rack housed about ten bottles, all of which had been positioned slightly forward so that their corks remained immersed in the wine. She returned with a bottle, two crystal glasses, and a wooden bottle opener. Without explanation, she carefully pulled the cork out so as not to disturb the wine, and then poured a delicate stream of pale, golden-hued liquid into each glass. "Taste it."

He lifted the glass to his lips. It seemed a long time before he murmured, "I've tasted this wine only once before." A spark of respect gleamed in his eyes as he glanced over at the bottle. A strange dark green in color, covered with a fine dust, the bottle bore the D'Asti's Private Stock Seal: a black falcon, the lithographed name of Andrea D'Asti, and a handwritten stock number. "This is your father's premium *pinot noir blanc* called The Eye of the Falcon, isn't it? It's a legend. But, tell me, why does it bear such an unusual name?"

"My father had hunting falcons in the old days. He decided to call this wine *L'occhio del falcone* after the glint in the eye of his favorite hunting bird."

So, there was a highly romantic streak in the D'Asti blood, after all. How much of this quality had she inherited? he wondered. His mind quickly snapped back to remembering when he had tasted this superb wine before. Then it came to him: Canova. Canova had invited him to share a bottle, all the while boasting how he had plotted and schemed to acquire it, and quoting over and over the fantastic price he had paid for the privilege of relishing this gem from old man D'Asti's private stock. This memory prodded Vic to remember also why he had come. Namely, business. "I hate to disillusion you, but as superb as this wine may be, you have only a few bottles left. Even if you auctioned off the remaining stock at the highest price, you still wouldn't have enough money to recoup your losses."

Laura looked faintly shocked. "I would never sell this wine! Papa gave some of it away to his very close friends, that's true, but the rest he left as a very special gift for me and Tina."

"Tina?" He tensed at the possibility of another obstacle.

"She's my kid sister." A hint of self-reproach passed over her lovely face. "She hates me to call her that, she's only a few years younger than I am. Tina's in her senior year at U.C. Davis where she's an enology and viticulture student." This time a loving smile broke through. "My sister's dead set on learning the science of the wine business and not having to learn it the hard way . . . the way I learned it."

He shook his head, saying seriously, "All the knowledge in the world won't save you, Laura. What this Winery needs is *money.*"

"That seems to be your favorite subject!" She couldn't hold back the anger anymore. Her voice broke with tension. Why was she allowing herself to go to pieces this way? What was so damned special about Vic Remo, anyway! "I thought somewhere deep inside of you there was a real love of wines, for the history and lore of the art. It seems I was wrong, the only thing you understand is hard facts! Well, I'm going to tell you a fact that will impress even your mercenary mind. Do you see those long rows of casks down the center of the cellars?" She signaled toward the area but never took her eyes off Vic's face.

"You mean the wine Matt Moyer was wasting his time and your money treating with bentonite? Oh, excuse me! I forgot that's the time-honored way to filter out the sediment, isn't it?" he asked with wicked wit.

"It's our way, yes! That's how we produce wines of the class you're so conspicuously savoring now!" This shot hit the mark, and she was glad. She had his complete attention now. "In those casks rests a wine that will surpass anything you've ever tasted. It will be more magnificent than even The Eye of the Falcon. I'm not talking about a few hundred bottles. Oh, no, I'm talking about much, much more!"

"Enough to save the Winery?"

"Yes!"

"In time to save the Winery? How will you pay the workers to do the work required to market this miracle of yours? Stop lying to yourself, Laura! You don't even have the money to harvest this year's vendange that's ripening out there in the fields. You've been forced to close the tasting room because you couldn't afford to keep it open to the public, I'll bet!"

"The workers will loyally stick by me. . . ."

"How long do you think that loyalty will last?"

"As long as it takes to save the wine!"

"You're dreaming. They have families to feed. It's not going to work."

"It must! Even if it doesn't, why should you care? I'm sure you can find another winery to devour. Why are so so hell bent on buying my Winery?"

Even if they hadn't been shouting at each other by this time, the vaulted ceilings of the cellars would have turned their sharp words into arrows. In the awful silence that followed, Vic finally told her, "I'm not interested in buying the Winery for myself. I'm representing a very large firm that's buying into the wine industry all over the valley, the Canova Corporation."

"Why should some large corporation want to grow grapes?"

"It's not interested in only growing grapes. The corporation's main interest is to invest its money in successful production to realize a substantial amount of money. It's as simple as that."

"That's horrible!" She was stunned. "You mean, you work for some huge, faceless company that just wants to make money and doesn't care anything about how long and how hard my family's worked to make fine wines? That's not only horrible, that's *disgusting*."

"No, it's practical." He took a firm grip on his rising temper. "It's also good economics, something you obviously know nothing about. And I happen to enjoy my work, especially since it's made me quite rich."

"Is that so? Well, you won't make a penny on *this* sale, Vic Remo, because"—the outrage she felt was directed at herself as much as at him—"I wouldn't sell this Winery to you or to your corporation even if I were starving!"

"That's your self-righteous D'Asti pride talking, not your common sense."

"Don't you dare use that condescending tone with me! I know what I'm talking about. You said it yourself a few minutes ago—I'm talking about loyalty. Don't laugh, Mr. Remo! Loyalty is the most important ingredient you'll find in those casks. I know because it broke my father's health and it cost my husband his life. I want you to go away and leave me alone!" Quickly, quickly, before the weak, stupid tears welled up and betrayed her. "Don't come back again, do you understand? I won't change my mind. I won't sell the Winery!"

Vic Remo must have left immediately because she still could hear the echo of her words when the door at the top of the stairs slammed shut. She couldn't remember the last time she had hated someone so much or felt such anger. She was shaking from head to toe. A shaft of light hit the prisms of the two crystal glasses, one empty, one full. The pale glint in The Eye of the Falcon winked back at her. "Stop lying to yourself, Laura. You'll die if you never see him again!"

CHAPTER TWO

"Thank you, Giorgio." Laura stepped out of the limousine. The chauffeur stood aside, cap in hand, showing a deference and politeness only generations could breed. He remained in this position until Laura and her sister crossed the wide sidewalk and reached halfway up the gleaming white steps leading to the formal entrance of the Memorial Opera House. Only then did he walk slowly back to the driver's side of the custom black Rolls, and despite the fact that limousines were waiting to occupy the reserved parking space, he drove off with unhurried respect for the masterpiece he was manipulating.

Laura hesitated, then gave in to the urge to turn and look at the street scene around her. The air was almost balmy at this hour of the early evening, blowing away the myth that San Francisco never had a summer. Over to the right, the last jewel had been set in the Civic Center's crown with the completion of the new Symphony Hall. Across the broad street now jammed with traffic stood the classic dome-lit City Hall. In the same architectural style, the building to the left housed the city's modern art collection. But the centerpiece of this panorama was the Opera House. Known throughout the world, the building's facade and pillars glowed with brilliance.

"I'm glad I drove home from college last night even though I had loads of studying to do. I wouldn't have missed this for the world," Tina confessed, gazing out over Laura's shoulder.

"I'm glad, too." Laura turned and smiled at her sister. This was the fourth opening gala Tina had attended with her since their father had died. Frank Spandoni had not cared for opera very much.

Something between a sigh and a giggle escaped from Tina. "One of my first childhood memories was your shrieks when Papa tried to take somebody else to the opera instead of you."

Laura took her sister by the arm and together they continued up the steps. "Yes, I guess I was a little bit of a devil about that." She laughed, also remembering the incident.

"There's still a little bit of the devil in you if you'd only let yourself break loose once in a while, Laura." Tina didn't like it when her sister became moody and introspective, something that had been happening too frequently lately. But she had really been frightened by Laura's behavior last night. She should have realized that something was wrong when she was rudely forced off the road leading up to the house by an oncoming sports car that must have been speeding at a hundred miles an hour. Of all the nerve! The second weird thing was finding Bella crouched on the front steps with her ears pulled back, a mad gleam in her eye, and her jaws snapping viciously at a white card in her mouth. Bella had coughed up the torn card on command, but then she had dashed into the house without even one wag of her tail in greeting. Strange! Tina tried to read the script on the mangled card, but all that was left was the name Vic Remo. Who the heck was that? she wondered. Most probably the lunatic that had forced her off the road!

She had called Laura's name throughout the silent house, but had received no response other than a hard snore from Donna Evangelina. Tina peeked into the front parlor and found the old woman snoozing in front of the fire as usual. Dressed in somber black from throat to foot, she looked as sour and cranky asleep as she did awake. Ugh! Tina had shuddered. She had never liked the old witch! Then, running from the house, she had literally stumbled over Matt Moyer. Why was he sitting alone in the gathering darkness? Always the gentlest of men, Matt had practically snapped her head off when she had asked if he knew where she could find Laura. "Off in the cellars," he had growled, where she had been fussing over some guy named Vic Remo. Had everybody suddenly gone nuts?

Tina had been almost hysterically relieved when she found Laura down in the cellars. That is, until she saw the tears and the pain in her sister's face. Shocked into silence, Tina realized she had never seen her sister cry, not even in moments of the most profound grief. Oh, yes, she remembered Laura's teen-age temper fits and shouts, but never had she seen her sister cry. Amazingly, Laura had offered no explanation for her bizarre tears, neither last night nor today, and Tina had wisely refrained from asking questions. Good thing, too, because Laura now seemed her usual serene, composed, beautiful self. Tina had no illusions, she knew she could never compete with her sister's calm beauty, although both had been blessed with the same lovely coloring and fine bone structure. What really set them apart was the difference in their personalities. Laura always seemed so unmoved, so calm, while Tina had the type of character others described as pert, bouncy, and inquisitive. For instance, she was itching to know what had really happened last night! Why had some guy named Vic Remo visited the Winery, and why had he left Laura in tears?

About to enter the Opera House, Laura thought of Tina's statement: "There's still a little bit of the devil in you if you'd only let yourself break loose once in a while." Better not explore the various possibilities of that, Laura decided. How could she explain last night without talking about Vic Remo? And how could she explain Vic Remo?

She passed through the doorway with Tina by her side. The marbled foyer was filled with the subdued murmurs of many voices, and Laura and Tina spent the next few minutes greeting friends and acquaintances. The distinguished director of the opera, a cherished family friend who had delighted the young Laura with irreverent renditions of some of opera's more ambiguous plots, smiled with adoration at the two sisters. "Ah, Lauretta, *carissima! E Titina, piccolina! Come felice sono che ambedue voi saresti cui ancora per cominciare nostra stagione nuova!*" With flair he welcomed them to the new season. Following Milanese protocol, he bestowed a fatherly kiss on Tina's forehead, but then bowed low over Laura's extended hand, kissing it with great affection.

"It looks like a wonderful season, *maestro. In bocca lupo!*" Laura lovingly wished him good luck by invoking the Italian theater's traditional warning to avoid the mouth of the wolf and not tempt fate.

"Laura! My God! You look simply gorgeous!"

Both Laura and Tina turned around at the sound of this familiar blast. Who else but brash, eccentric, wonderful Lucy? Lucy Kaye had a small spread, as she liked to call her thousand-acre ranch, near the D'Asti property, and although she was twenty years older than Laura, they were the best of friends and confidantes. Whenever Laura came down to San Francisco, Lucy always insisted on playing hostess. In fact, the two sisters were spending the weekend at Lucy's posh town house in Pacific Heights. Trying hard not to smile, Laura saw that her friend was, as usual, hopelessly overdressed. Lucy was sporting something luridly purple accented with great splotches of red and topped off by a pink scarf that was in furious conflict with her constant movements. The entire effect was that of a somewhat dumpy tropical bird preparing to take flight.

"Thanks for the compliment, Lucy, but this gown's hardly new, you know. You've seen me wear it before."

"Maybe." Lucy nodded, inspecting Laura with a keen eye. Could anybody ever believe that the young woman working like a drudge in cutoffs and tank tops in the vineyards of Sonoma was the same person as this vision standing here? From the shining coil of bronze-flecked hair smoothed back from the beautiful face to the simple floor-length black sheath that left neck, shoulders, and just the top roundness of her breasts bare and the white moiré silk shawl draped loosely around one arm and left to trail behind on the floor, Laura was the picture of assured elegance. "Maybe, honey, but no matter what you wear and how often you wear it, you somehow always manage to look like an empress. It's just your style, Laura. Now, I look like an unmade bed no matter what I wear, so I just have fun and indulge my fantasies! How do you like my outfit? I bought it at a secondhand bargain shop somewhere in the Mission District!"

"You're outrageous! But don't ever change, Lucy. I like you just as you are." Laura laughed. "Oh, before I forget, thanks so much for sending Giorgio and your Rolls back to the town house for us this evening."

"My pleasure. But why didn't you want to come with me earlier to attend that marvelous pre-opera champagne party in the Green Room? I think Tina would have loved it. Hello, pet!" she said, hugging Tina to her full bosom. "You look lovely, too. Ah, youth!" A second later, she studiously repeated her question. "Why didn't you come to the party, Laura?"

"I don't like champagne." She said the first thing that popped into her mind.

"That sounds like a bum excuse to me." Lucy peered at Laura a little more closely. Could it be that something was boiling away underneath that calm surface?

"It's not just an excuse. I . . ."

"It *is* an excuse," Tina interrupted, taking the plunge before she lost her nerve. She would never have dared speak up if Lucy hadn't been there. "Admit it, Laura, you've been awfully moody lately."

"Really, Tina, I don't think this is the time or place . . ."

"When is it ever the right time and place for you to unload? Oh, I know you still think of me as your baby sister! You're always trying to protect me, as if I didn't know anything about life." She sniffed and turned toward Lucy, pleading, "You're her best friend, maybe she'll open up to you. Maybe she'll tell you why last night . . ."

"Tina!" Suddenly, the warning signal that the opera was

about to begin rang out. With obvious relief, Laura turned to climb one of the side staircases. "We'd better hurry to our seats. Will you come upstairs during intermission, Lucy?"

"Sure, sure. We'll meet by the bar in the grand foyer."

Laura had almost reached the top of the angled steps, so she missed the look that passed between Tina and Lucy. "Was that really necessary, Tina?"

"I think so." They were walking rapidly and talking in whispers. Tina put her hand out, catching Laura's fingers before she could open the door leading to their seats. "Laura, what's the matter?"

"Nothing! Let's forget everything else and enjoy this performance, all right?" Laura turned the gilded door handle and walked through the small Regency anteroom decorated in pale damask. She nodded and smiled to the others already seated and then took her place in one of the two front seats of Box Six. Tina quickly took the other seat. There was just enough time for one last meaningful glance between the sisters before the lights began to dim in the beautiful cream-and-gold opera house. Applause greeted the entrance of the conductor, and after a few coughs and general murmurs, the sweet strains of the Overture to *La traviata* began.

"Concentrate on the music," Laura told herself. "You love this opera, so concentrate on every note!" But she couldn't. She found her mind wandering and her eyes wandered, too, even after the curtain had lifted and the music, singing, and action started to unfold in the timeless love story. Just below on the orchestra level it wasn't hard to spot Lucy, whose plumage stuck out like a splashy rainbow amid the tasteful background of white furs and black ties. She was seated with the ladies and gentlemen of the press because although fabulously rich Lucy didn't believe in being fabulously idle. She was the proud owner of the *Sonoma Sundial,* and her chief joy was writing her paper's society column.

Laura's eyes continued to flicker around the audience. Everybody at this gala appeared so self-satisfied, so well-to-do. Was there anybody else in this house, she wondered, who had put off buying a new piece of farm equipment in order to pay for this season's tickets—as she had? A foolish extravagance perhaps, but then she also doubted if anyone else had personally spent hours picking out just the right seats when this house was built over forty years ago, as her grandfather had done. Ever since, through good and bad times, the D'Astis had occupied the first two seats of Box Six for the entire opera season, year in, year out. She knew she wasn't the only one who had sacrificed for this privilege. Tina had really applied herself at college and had been awarded a fine scholarship, taking some of the pressure off the dwindling D'Asti bank account, thank God! Laura's thoughts caused her to glance fondly at her sister's profile when a brilliant flash in the darkness beyond captured her eye. Several boxes ahead, a very attractive blonde sat languidly watching the stage with half-closed eyes. Laura continued to gaze at her for two reasons: First, she had never seen this woman before in that particular box, and then she was wearing the costliest, most luscious diamond necklace imaginable. Each gem was so large, so sparkling that Laura thought the jewels must be fake. But on second thought, no chic female in her right mind would wear such an impossibly huge piece of fake jewelry. No, it had to be the real thing. Mindful she had been openly staring, Laura shifted her eyes instantly to the stage. The soprano and tenor had just reached that part of the score where the young lovers-to-be raised glasses of champagne to each other in the celebrated *Bríndisi,* and the sight of the pale golden wine in those glasses jarred something loose in Laura's memory that she had been fighting desperately to bury since last night. With a will of their own, her eyes darted back to the chic blonde, but this time it wasn't the gorgeous necklace that held her spellbound. A man whose face and shoulders were blocked from Laura's view by other persons seated in between slowly placed his arm around the back of the blond woman's chair. There was more than enough light reflected from the lavish stage setting to highlight little details on his dark sleeve, such as the four small buttons near the cuff, but Laura wasn't interested in such trivia. It was what she saw below the man's cuff that was so startling—a slim band of gold on the wrist, and just below that, a familiar white bandage. It had to be a coincidence. Except why was she suddenly trembling? If she had obeyed her instincts and averted her eyes immediately, she wouldn't have seen Vic Remo shift in his chair somewhat impatiently, and she wouldn't have watched as he absent-mindedly scanned faces inevitably to find hers. At first, she was sure he didn't recognize her. His eyes seemed merely to sparkle polite male approval. It took a few seconds longer, seconds during which the enchanting melody of the love duet was being sung on a stage somewhere far away, before his gaze changed from admiration to astonishment. Laura didn't smile, and she didn't turn her head away. In fact, she did nothing to make this moment easier for him or for herself. She couldn't. She was as amazed to see him as he obviously was to see her. Had it been only yesterday that they had faced each other in anger? What diabolic twist of fate had thrown them together again here of all places, and so soon, too? A nervous premonition had filled her since the moment she had stepped into the opera house, and now she finally knew why.

Neither of them seemed to be aware of anything or anyone else. They were aware only of each other. Vic's glamorous companion felt his arm slipping away, and she peered over her shoulder at him, surprised. Receiving no response, she followed his eyes. . . .

"Laura! Why are you just sitting there? Wasn't that some of the most thrilling singing you've ever heard?"

Dazed, blinking slightly at the bright lights, Laura saw Tina standing, applauding jubilantly. The exciting *Sempre libera* aria that ended the first act must have been superbly sung by the diva because the rest of the audience was applauding just as enthusiastically.

"Yes, yes, it was beautiful . . ." Laura stood up, feeling alarmed. She hadn't heard a note of the aria, not a single, solitary note! The applause continued on and on, grating on her ears and on her nerves. Finally, after what seemed an eternity, the curtain calls stopped, and everyone headed for the grand foyer.

"Oh, what a mob! We'll never find Lucy in this crush," Tina said as soon as they arrived at the bar.

"I really doubt she's made it up here yet. Come on, let's wait for her at the other end of the foyer." Laura had good reason to avoid the bar. She had just seen Vic and the blonde; the one thing she didn't want to do was to talk to him now. She had to have time to clear the fuzziness from her head and pull herself together. Just as Laura had predicted, Lucy finally appeared, short of breath from the short climb up the stairs and shaking her head in disbelief. "All that whooping and hollering is enough to drive anybody up the wall! How can the two of you seriously admit you enjoy listening to all that noise? I'm telling you the honest truth, I hate opera!"

"Then why on earth do you punish yourself by coming here to listen to it?" Tina asked, bursting with laughter.

"Because culture brings out all the beautiful people. That's what I write about in my society column, remember? The beautiful and the rich. I've already spotted some very interesting people...."

"Tina, the crowd at the bar seems to be thinning, and this poor woman looks like she could use a drink. Would you get Lucy some champagne?" Laura didn't enjoy being devious, but she had something important to ask Lucy, something she didn't want Tina to hear.

"Oh, that would save my life!" Lucy bellowed.

"Sure." Tina smiled. "Anything for you, Laura? I know you don't want champagne...." She was being pert again.

"No, thanks."

As soon as Tina had left, Lucy got right to the point. "All right, now that you've gotten rid of your kid sister on that trumped up errand of mercy, maybe you'll tell me what's on your mind."

Lucy was sharp, and Laura knew it. "It's nothing important, really. I wanted to know the name of that attractive blonde standing over there at the bar."

Lucy peered over in that direction, squinting a lot. "Sure, I know her." She turned back to Laura. "I've never known you to get your kicks following the exploits of the jet set. Why the sudden interest in that particular bundle of money?"

"She's very pretty . . . and she's wearing such fabulous jewelry...." Laura broke off lamely. Well, she had really flubbed that one!

"Yeah, that's some hunk of ice cubes she has hanging

around her neck, isn't it? That's Carole Canova." Lucy's curiosity was further sharpened by Laura's reaction to the name. She wasn't just impressed; she was outright stunned. What kind of game was Laura playing, anyway? Lucy wondered. Whatever it was, she fully intended to get a handle on this puzzle, so she kept talking while watching Laura like a hawk. "She's the much-married, much-divorced daughter of Ricardo Canova. You know, he's the banking and investments czar. It might interest you to know that Papa Canova has been snatching up a lot of land in the Napa-Sonoma area lately. Anyway, he can afford it! He bought his darling little baby Carole that itsy-bitsy trinket she's sporting as a reward for being a good girl and ridding herself of her latest matrimonial disaster. Ex-husband number four was some kind of organic creep who ate nothing but air! Just goes to show the crazy things a poor little rich girl will do to keep herself from being bored to death, eh?" Her tone became a bit more confidential. "But my inside sources tell me darling Carole's main problem isn't just healthy boredom. It seems her libido got thrown out of wack somewhere down the line, and underneath all that glamor Carole Canova's just your nice, average, normal nympho. . . ."

"That's probably only malicious gossip," Laura said much too strongly. Why was she defending someone she didn't even know? But it wasn't that simple. No, it wasn't Carole Canova's unsavory reputation against which she was protesting.

"Oh, I don't think so. My sources are usually pretty reliable. Anyhow, it'll be fascinating to see if Vic Remo becomes husband number five. But I'm betting he's too smart to get caught in her clutches."

"Vic Remo?" Murmuring his name was about as far as Laura could trust herself.

"He's that incredibly handsome guy standing there with Carole." Lucy's ears had caught something in Laura's voice she couldn't quite pinpoint. "Don't tell me you haven't noticed him?" It wasn't a question; it was more an accusation. "God knows, every other woman in this place has batted her false eyelashes at him at least once tonight!"

"I've noticed him."

Lucy allowed herself an unladylike snort. "I've known Vic since he was a youngster. Haven't I told you about him before?"

"No."

"Vic's worked his way up the ladder of success the hard way, and he's become a renowned expert in the wine business. He's a top executive with the Canova Corporation, but he's strictly his own man, know what I mean? Oh, sure, he's as ambitious as hell, but there's something about the guy that makes me respect and admire him."

Respect and admire? Those were two words Laura couldn't imagine using to describe Vic Remo! Maybe he had managed to pull the wool over Lucy's eyes, but he hadn't fooled *her*. There was no denying he had charm and looks, and he could wreck a woman's self-control with a single spark from those dusky eyes. But she knew he was probably nothing more than a calculating, cold-blooded opportunist. No wonder he could boast about enjoying his work so much—what man couldn't with such beautiful and sexy fringe benefits!

"Oh, my! It looks like things aren't going too smoothly for our haughty, spoiled glamor queen," Lucy said, nodding toward the bar. Laura didn't want to hear or see anything. However, Lucy's second "Oh, my!" really couldn't be ignored. Laura glanced over just as Vic was turning away from the bar. He was holding two glasses, and he offered one to Carole. He must have said something to upset her, because she refused the champagne with a violent snap of her head. She continued to stare at him with absolute venom, and then she spat out a vulgar word and walked away in a rage.

Neither Carole's language nor her absence seemed to bother Vic very much. His only apparent dilemma seemed to be what to do with the two glasses still in his hands. As luck would have it, Tina happened to be standing a few feet away, still waiting for the bartender to take her order. Vic hardly hesitated; with charming courtesy, he smiled at Tina and handed over the two glasses.

It took only a second for Tina to come rushing back to Laura and Lucy, absolutely thrilled. "Do you know what just happened to me? I was standing at the bar, minding my own business, and this divine, dreamy hunk of a guy just handed me these two glasses!"

"We know, we saw it all," Lucy soothed, helping herself to one of the glasses. "I was just telling your sister some fascinating facts about that dreamy hunk. His name's Vic Remo."

Tina choked loudly on her champagne. "Say, that's the guy who went to see you at the Winery yesterday, Laura. Matt Moyer told me."

Laura closed her eyes not only to shut out Lucy's dumbfounded stare, but also because Vic Remo was striding toward her. She had to conquer this uneasiness, that's all there was to it! After all, what harm could he do to her? He was just like any other man, wasn't he? But hearing his mellow voice with that hint of forcefulness in it instantly undermined her resolve.

"How are you, Lucy? Still snooping around for that gossip column of yours?" He gave her a fond kiss on the top of her head. "I know you're not here because you're a music lover."

"Darned right, I'm not." She laughed, hugging him back, taking the swift shift of events in stride. "Anyway, my readers really relish my tales. I tell you one thing, I'm really going to wow them with my vivid version of that scene I just witnessed between you and the notorious Carole Canova!"

Vic's nonchalant shrug clearly stated his lack of interest in the whole affair. Instead, he turned his attention to Tina. "You're Tina D'Asti, aren't you?"

"Yes, yes, I am. But how did you know?"

"Your sister told me a lot about you yesterday." He slowly turned his head. "Hello, Laura."

"Hello, Vic," she said with surprising calm.

"Well, well," Lucy put in. "I didn't know you and *my dear friend* Laura knew each other!" Her voice dripped with sweetness. "Wait a minute. What happened to your hand, Vic? Don't tell me you finally drove one of your adoring girl friends bananas? Did the poor darling go wild and start chewing on your hand?"

He held up the bandaged hand and laughed. "To tell you the truth, it was something like that, wasn't it, Laura?"

"Nothing quite so melodramatic, I would say. The bandage has been changed. Did you go to a doctor?"

"No, of course not. The wound's almost healed, so I just put this small gauze around it myself."

"I don't understand. Did this happen yesterday at the Winery?" Tina asked.

They had been speaking in a polite, civil manner, and

Laura was proud of the way she had resisted looking squarely at Vic. But now she made the mistake of glancing up and saw the teasing glint in his eye and the smile beginning to take hold of his full mouth. The image of the silly fracas by the pond with the squawking and feathers flying and pushing and pulling came back to her in a flash. She just couldn't help it, she began to laugh, too. "It was all Bella's fault, and it was all so stupid!"

"Since Bella's not here to defend herself, why don't we forget the whole thing," Vic said. "You're not drinking anything, Laura. Can I get you some champagne?"

Still laughing a little, she shook her head. "No, thank you."

"Laura doesn't like champagne," Tina volunteered, sly as a puss. "Didn't she tell you that yesterday?"

"No, somehow we never got around to discussing champagne." Vic was serious now, but there was a certain warm appeal in his gaze that Laura couldn't overlook. "Unlike my friend Lucy here, I think you like opera very much, don't you, Laura?"

"Yes, I've loved it since I was a child."

"How many times have you seen *La traviata?* Five times maybe, even more?"

"Mm-m-m, many more times. Why?"

"Skip the rest of the performance and have dinner with me, instead."

It was such an unthinkable, crazy idea that Laura gasped. Why was it every time she let her guard down, even just a little, this man always sensed it? "I wouldn't dream of leaving. . . ." The warning signal rang out, and the intermission was over.

"I have a small restaurant in mind I think you'll like very much. It's my favorite place in San Francisco." He spoke softly, but the hidden challenge was there, nevertheless—*are you afraid of me, Laura?* "Lucy, you wouldn't mind dropping Tina off after the opera wherever she's staying, would you?"

"Laura and Tina are staying with me this weekend."

"Is that so? Then taking Tina home would be no problem, would it?"

"Oh . . . oh, no problem at all! Of course! Come on, pet," Lucy coaxed none too subtly, dragging Tina headlong down the foyer.

The cold marbled foyer was quiet now; only faint drifts of music could be heard coming from inside the opera house. Vic and Laura were the only people left, and they weren't saying anything. Finally Vic held out his hand and waited. Laura let her fingers slip into his strong hand and they slowly descended the staircase.

CHAPTER THREE

Everything whizzed by in an unseen blur, the lights, the streets, the buildings, and the people. Laura kept her head turned sharply toward the window, but she was paying scant attention to anything outside the confines of the sportscar.

"I think we should call a truce, don't you? I promise not to make any mention of the Winery, and you stop treating me like some kind of sworn enemy." Vic thrust the shift into low gear, and the car quickly accelerated up the steep street.

Holding on fiercely to the leather dashboard, Laura waited until they arrived at the crest before she looked directly at him. "That will be difficult, won't it? Calling a truce, I mean. Can either of us forget yesterday?"

"It's easy. I've already forgotten. Yesterday never happened to us. "We met tonight for the first time. I saw you there in the darkness, and you saw me. We both liked what we saw." His voice was so low that the hum of the motor threatened to cover his words. He began to edge the car down the other side of the hill. "It could work for us, Laura, if you would only give it half a chance."

Could it happen so simply? she wondered. Could they erase all memory of the anger they had flung at each other? And what about the specter of the Winery? Still, she was here. He hadn't physically pulled her from the opera house, had he? No, she had wanted to be with him. "We met tonight for the first time . . ." Why not?

"All right," she declared with dry humor, "I now call a truce between Vic Remo and Laura D'Asti! At least, for tonight, anyway. All we know about one another is that you live in this city and that I live out in the country." She liked the way he reached for her hand, gripping it almost too tightly. So he was impulsive, too! Beneath that veneer of rigid self-control he was hiding something about himself, she realized. Perhaps she had been too harsh when she had called him cold-blooded and calculating. His fingers felt warm and good and honest, but she couldn't read his face. Bending her head forward slightly, she asked, "By the way, what does Vic stand for?"

"We'll have to be much better friends before I'll tell you that secret," he said, laughing.

They had just entered the Stockton Street tunnel and the white tiled interior shone with the lights of the traffic. The reflections reminded Laura of the sparkle of rubies and diamonds. *Diamonds!* "Won't Carole Canova wonder where you are?"

"She might, but it doesn't matter. She'll have no problem finding somebody to take her home."

His answer was blunt enough, but his grip tightened around her fingers. "Let it be," Laura warned herself, *"and change the subject quickly."* "If you won't tell me your real name, won't you at least tell me about this restaurant you like so much? I'm really curious. What's so special about it?"

"The food's great, but there's nothing grand or pretentious about the place. Actually it's just a small neighborhood *trattoria* that serves jug wine. Do you mind?" He stole time from the heavy traffic to cast a teasing glance in her direction.

"No, of course not! But I still think there must be something special about it, or it wouldn't be your favorite. Let's face it, San Francisco is rather famous for its Italian restaurants!"

Traffic was a mess at the end of the tunnel as it neared the North Beach section, and when he finally had a chance to talk he asked instead, "Do you like authentic Sicilian cooking?" He laughed at the quizzical look on her face. "You're probably not familiar with southern Italy's cooking, are you? I remember you said your family came from one of the northern provinces."

He remembered that tiny bit of information, did he? "Yes, we were originally from Tuscany. Is the food really that different?"

"As different as night and day, just like the customs and the language. The people are different, too." He lifted her hand slightly as if to underscore his point. Even in the semidarkness his dark skin shadowed her fairer hand. "We also love stronger."

She almost protested the truth of that remark, but she wasn't too sure he wasn't teasing her again. No doubt he considered himself an expert on love, too. Still, she missed the hard pressure of that dark hand as he constantly shifted gears, weaving through the congestion along Columbus in the heart of North Beach. He shared his thoughts with her, though, and that kept the intimacy alive. "You can always tell the tourists from the natives, can't you?" he said, nodding at the swarms of people laughing and enjoying themselves as they walked about the streets. "I remember when this area still fancied itself as bohemian as the Left Bank of Paris." He suddenly braked sharply, narrowly avoiding a young couple who had stopped in the center of the street to exchange a smoldering, passionate kiss. His hand shot out to protect Laura against the car's screeching halt. "You okay?" Reassured, he sighed, shook his head good-naturedly, and worked the car around the lovers who remained locked together in blissful oblivion. "I've seen this neighborhood pass through the phase of the flower children, too, but I wonder what it must have been like back in the infamous days of the Barbary Coast. Wilder than this, I'll bet. It's still an exciting area, though, mostly because of the mixed nationalities—Portuguese, Corsicans, Asians, Mexicans, and Italians from Genoa, Milan, Naples, and Sicily. Ah, here's my favorite church." He drove past a lovely gold-and-white facade. "That's Saint Peter and Saint Paul."

He continued alongside Washington Square and then followed one of the narrow one-way streets at the base of Telegraph Hill. The road was steep, and cars were parked haphazardly all over the place. He stopped the car in the middle of the street, rotating the wheels so that the front right tire wedged against one of the antispeeding concrete bars dotting the surface of the street. Still, the car seemed in danger of sliding down the street again. "Here we are. Let me help you out."

Laura was surprised. Did he intend to leave this expensive car like this? But she had no time to dwell on this problem. She felt herself pulled effortlessly onto the sidewalk. The balminess of the early evening had given way to San Francisco's notorious wind, and a sudden gust threw her off balance. Her thin shawl whipped around her body, and her arms were instantly pinned to her sides. Vic instinctively reached out to hold her. Swaying precariously within his arms, she looked around for a sign of a restaurant. All she could see was a large food market with the legend *Buzzano da Messina* emblazoned across its window. Some wisps of hair fanned themselves across her eyes, and she shook her head to clear them away. "Where's the restaurant?" Unable to move, she was aware his arms had slipped down to her waist. But it didn't matter; his arms felt good there.

"It's behind the market."

"*Behind* the market?" Her delicate evening slippers had not been designed for climbing hills in a gale, and she was bending closer and closer to him for support. "I don't believe it!"

"But it's true."

She searched his face for the small smile that would tell her this was all a joke. But he wasn't smiling. His full mouth had parted and he might have murmured, "Laura. . . ." Perhaps he would kiss her; she very badly wanted him to kiss her.

When she finally felt the caress, it didn't fall against her mouth, but across the wisps of her hair. Unable to grasp his head, she lifted her face upward, searching for his mouth. . . .

"Hey, Vic!"

Vic moved a little away, cursing softly. A curly-haired kid came running out of the market. He wore a very large white apron over his jeans and a very wide grin. "I didn't expect to see you tonight, friend!" He gave Laura a frank once-over and showed his approval with an even wider grin. "Want me to park the car in your garage, Vic?"

"Sure," he murmured, flipping the keys over to the kid. "Why don't you do that, Joe." The youngster jumped in the car and drove off like a bat out of hell, still grinning. "You're shivering," Vic whispered to Laura. "Come on, let's go inside out of this wind, and I'll prove to you I wasn't lying about that restaurant."

Laura let Vic guide her to the door of the market, her mind in a whirl. How odd! She could have sworn the boy said he would park the car in Vic's garage. Perhaps she was mistaken. Perhaps she was mistaken about a lot of things. Faith in her own common sense had been badly shaken. Here she was trembling, not because of the winds, but because of reasons she couldn't even begin to fathom. She was actually eager to let herself be enticed by Vic's dynamic personality, even to the extent of dallying on a romantic windswept corner of Telegraph Hill, yearning for a kiss like a moonstruck teenybopper! For God's sake!

But the evening's surprises were not over yet. Laura stepped into the warm, friendly market and the past came rushing back. How many years had gone by since she had been inside a totally European market like this one? She was immediately filled with an almost overwhelming nostalgia.

"I know it's unorthodox," Vic confessed, "but we get to the restaurant by walking to the rear of the market. . . ."

"Oh, please! Can I have just a moment to look around?"

"Of course." Vic was beginning to realize she was a woman whose moods changed quickly.

"This place brings back such *wonderful* memories."

"Memories of what, Laura?"

"We always bought all our supplies in a market very much like this somewhere down by the wharf." She began to walk down the main aisle, picking up and gazing at various packets of food displayed in large barrels. "We would come down from Sonora three or four times a year, have all the food bundled in sacks and crates, and then everything would be piled on the back of our flatbed truck for the long trip home. I loved every hour we spent together, choosing exactly what we needed. Then would come the best thing of all. We would always reward ourselves by buying a cold lemon ice. It was silly, but we ate it very slowly, hoping it would last forever. Then I would curl up on his shoulder on the drive home, and I would almost always fall asleep before we had passed the San Francisco city limits. Sometimes I didn't wake up until I heard the shouts greeting our return to the Winery. Awake or asleep, he always held me so lovingly."

"Welcome back, Laura."

"What?" Laura felt the strong, possessive hold on her hand, and she saw Vic standing there. She was confused for a second.

"You were reliving the past with your husband."

"No, I wasn't," she murmured. "I was with my father." She gently pulled her hand away and continued to stroll along the aisles filled with Italian imports. "Mama never cooked a meal for less than twenty people. We would have huge formal dinners after church on Sunday, and it was always a tradition to have guests for supper on Wednesday evening, also." She found a side panel stocked with different grains ranging in color from the palest white to the richest yellow. "Even our weekday breakfasts were something special." She laid her fingertips on a glass drawer marked *farina di polenta*. The flour within was a glorious yellow. "Mama would make large trays of this baked in the oven. When it was all fluffy—oh, how *good* it smelled—she would cut it into squares and serve it with warm milk and cinnamon sprinkled over the top. Tina loved her *polenta* when she was a baby."

Laura looked around at the abundance of black olives, cured hams, nuts, glazed candies, and, hanging from the ceiling, the salamis and the cheeses. Of course, the place of honor was saved to display the infinite variety of pasta. Laura ran over to read the names. "*Cannelloni, manicotti, lasagna, fettuccine, tagliarini, cavatelli, rigatoni, mostaccioli.*" She laughed, out of breath. "Don't they sound like names from some comic opera?"

"Yes, they do," Vic said lightly, adjusting to her whimsical train of thought. "Tell me the truth now. Which is your favorite?"

"None of these." It was her turn to tease. "Mama always made her own pasta. It didn't make any difference in what shape it appeared on our table for supper—if we ate pasta, it had been made fresh in our kitchen that morning."

Laura suddenly shook her head. "How awful! I was reliving the past and that's sick and unhealthy!"

"No, it's not. What's wrong with remembering the past?"

"It hurts too much, that's what!"

Vic placed his fingers gently over her lips to stop the words. People were shopping along the aisles, yet nobody seemed to notice the elegantly dressed, handsome couple, conversing intimately by the side wall. San Franciscans were by nature immune to almost anything, and tourists rarely ventured into this type of neighborhood store.

When Vic's fingers parted, Laura was smiling with a

nonchalance an experienced actress would have envied. "Vic, I'm hungry! Where is that damned restaurant, anyway?"

There was nothing he could do but play her game. "The entrance is there, behind you. Suddenly I'm hungry, too."

He led her through a doorway leading from the market into the *trattorìa* and instantly received a warm and familiar greeting from a man who could only be the owner of the small, cozy café. Introduced to Laura as "Dario, my cousin," the owner opened his arms in a wide welcome and waved them over to the *tavola calda*, a long counter heaped with large oval dishes bearing an assortment of prepared foods. "Choose what you want as a starter, and then Dario will bring the rest of the meal to our table," Vic said.

Laura inspected the dishes and then quickly made a wise decision. "You were right, everything is cooked differently. Oh, Vic, please help me!"

"I should punish you."

"Why?"

"For being skeptical when I told you there were differences between us. I should let you go hungry."

"But you wouldn't do that, would you?" There was a tautness around his mouth that was as exciting to Laura as it was surprising.

"No, only because I'm all heart. I'll choose for both of us, and I'll explain as we go along."

She slipped her hands around his arm. It wasn't her imagination; she unmistakably felt the tension all along his body at her touch. "I'm truly repentant, I swear it. Carry on, Mr. Remo."

She purposely didn't let go of him, but she paid close attention as he pointed out first one dish and then another.

"That's raw eggplant marinated in olive oil and garlic, and these are artichoke hearts that have been rolled in cheese and then fried. Here we have red peppers baked, skinned, and preserved in wine vinegar, and those are cubes of fresh veal garnished with creamed spinach. Ah, here's one of my favorites, rice, first boiled, then rolled in a mixture of bread crumbs and cheese, then baked till the crust turns beautiful. . . ." The list went on and on, and he hadn't even touched upon the fish dishes, which featured delicacies ranging from braised mussels to cod baked in a sauce of tomatoes, onions, and black olives.

"Enough!" Laura protested. "Please! That's more than enough."

Dario held two very full plates over the counter and shrugged. "A pigeon, it would starve on this diet! But go, sit down, and I'll serve you with hot dishes when you have finished this. *Buon gusto!*"

Balancing a dish in each hand, Vic took Laura to a side table set with a simple tablecloth and a single candle. The cafe was quiet and private, and the other patrons seemed more interested in their own suppers than in watching Laura and Vic. A group of college kids were energetically wolfing down pasta and discussing the plus and minuses of last night's punk-rock concert, while in another corner some colorful North Beach natives, nattily dressed in old-style suits and ties topped by berets and caps, were debating the finer moments of this afternoon's *bocce* ball game. Their Neapolitan accents were thick, *sótto vóce*, and merry. They seemed to be slightly tipsy. Neighborhood papers published in Italian occupied the attention of several others who were comfortably eating and drinking.

Vic poured some deep red wine from a ceramic jug into

Laura's glass. "This stuff was on the vine yesterday, but it's good. How's the food?"

"Marvelous. I don't *quite* know what I'm eating, but it tastes great." She drank some of the wine. "This is good, too. Were you afraid I wouldn't like this café, Vic? Do you really think I'm that much of a snob?"

But Vic never had a chance to answer. Dario arrived, pushing a cart containing a number of chafing dishes, and they had a spirited exchange in a strong Sicilian dialect about the remainder of the feast. The only words Laura could really understand were *mostaccioli* and *salsa arrabbiata*. Immediately, a combination of tubular pasta and fiery tomato sauce appeared on their plates. "Oh, this is spicy," she said, barely tasting it, "and delicious, but I honestly can't eat another bite." She noticed Vic had hardly touched his food, and the plate of pasta was pushed aside, too. A frown hooded his eyes, and she was sorry she had asked such a stupid question. Why should he think she was a snob? "You said you were hungry, remember?"

"Did I?" He leaned back in his chair and drank the wine. "Perhaps I was, but I'm not now." The frown disappeared and his lips began to curl up at the corners. "I'll apologize to Dario tomorrow. He takes it as a personal insult when people don't lick their plates clean."

"Is he really your cousin?"

"Oh, yes, and his brother owns the market." The smile grew. "I'm surrounded by cousins."

"Did you all grow up together here in San Francisco?"

"No, we grew up worlds apart. When my parents married, they said good-bye to the family in Sicily and started a new life in this city. I very literally grew up right here on this spot."

"Here? I don't understand."

"This is where we had our small vegetable store."

The twinkle in his eye was irresistible, and she found herself responding to him in a way that was almost alarming. "I should have guessed!" Suddenly she wanted to know everything about his childhood and his life. "Do your parents still live in the neighborhood?"

He shook his head. "Funny how it all turned out. Although they loved California, I think my parents had promised each other that they would return to their homeland someday. But money was scarce, and they both had the crazy dream that I had to go to college, so it took a few years before I could afford to send them back to Sicily. That's one of the good things about having money," he murmured, refilling both wineglasses. "It feels good when you can spend as much as you want on people you really care a hell of a lot about."

She searched for some hint of sarcasm, but there wasn't any. "You were responsible for bringing your cousins over, too, weren't you?"

"Yes." He took a sip of wine. "We traded, actually. My parents took over the old family house in Sicily and Dario took over this property. We bought the adjacent buildings on this block, built up the store, and added this *trattorìa*. I've also added every possible modern convenience to the old house in Sicily. Now everybody is happy."

"What about you?" She would never have guessed that generosity was part of his nature, and she had almost slipped badly. To have asked if he was happy would have been just plain snooping. "I mean, don't you miss not seeing your parents?"

"I fly over there two or three times a year." His expressive fingers circled the rim of his glass several times. "You'd like the view from our old house, Laura. It's up on a hill, and below lies a valley that looks very much like your valley. The weather's about the same, too." A wry smile chased away whatever he might have been thinking. "Otherwise, the two places have absolutely nothing in common! You're not drinking your wine."

"I . . . I don't want anymore, thank you."

"Coffee?"

Laura didn't want any coffee, but she didn't want to leave the quiet sanctuary of this little café, either. Perhaps more than anything else, she didn't want to do or say anything that might destroy the fragile thread of intimacy and understanding that was binding them together. The college crowd had broken into pairs and settled down to more romantic pursuits and most of the old men had left, so nothing could really break the peaceful spell that surrounded the two of them.

"Laura . . . ?"

"Yes, I'd like some coffee."

He pushed away from the table. "Fine. We'll have it at my place."

To protest would be childish, she knew. "All right." She hesitated only because she dreaded facing the cold wind again. At least, that's what she told herself. "It's so quiet and comfortable here."

"It's quiet and comfortable in my apartment, too." He lifted her shawl and wrapped it lightly around her bare shoulders. "I live nearby, you won't get cold."

Another surprise. "Really? I just assumed . . ."

"Assumed what? That I lived in some prized showplace at the Marina?"

"Frankly, that's exactly what I thought."

"I don't follow the rules, I make my own. Haven't you figured that out yet, Laura?"

He didn't give her much of a chance to ponder that question; they were through the doorway and into the market in a wink. Bobbing up from behind a stack of *citroni dolci* boxes, young Joe handed back Vic's keys. "That car of yours really rides!" Showing off his brash know-how in such matters, he added, "You really should have those cams checked."

"I will," Vic promised, indulging the kid's ego.

Dario was busy helping out behind the delicatessen counter, but he stopped his work immediately and came around to say good-bye. *"Ciao, cugino!"* he said, slapping Vic fondly on the back. "And you, signorina, you will come back, eh? Even if my cousin is too busy to bring you himself, you will come again?"

"I certainly will come back." Laura liked the man as much as she liked his little restaurant. "I promise."

The air outside was chilly and turbulent, but Vic, true to his word, led her only a few paces up the hill to a venerable sandstone house. They dashed quickly up the many steps, and when he opened the front door, she was confronted with another of the evening's surprises. Solid oak gleamed everywhere with a patina only loving care and costly preservation could maintain. They were standing in a small vestibule. He opened one of the doors along the side wall. "It's humble, but it's home."

His "humble home" reflected his personality perfectly, she realized, slightly awed by what she was seeing. Masculine, subdued, understated, the apartment also revealed his sensitivity. And yes, his temperament.

"We need a fire," he said. Slowly he began to pull the shawl away from her body, and she felt the searing effect of the contact of his hands upon her skin. It was all over in a moment, however. He let the shawl fall on a nearby brown silk chair, and then he moved away from her. She wasn't even sure he had stroked the bare flesh along her neck and her back; perhaps she had only felt the gossamer softness of the shawl.

It was pleasurable also to watch him coax warm flames out of the large logs resting in the fireplace that covered an entire wall. It was unadorned except for the sensuous grains always found in real Carrara marble.

She turned and walked slowly across the enchanting room, enjoying the things that belonged to him: the Chinese woodcuts on the walls; the complex stereo system surrounded by a vast collection of records and tapes, running the gamut from the earliest operas of Monteverdi to traditional New Orleans jazz; the comfortable chairs and sofa done in warm earth-tone velvet; the books; the personal items such as the collection of pipes and tobacco jars lined in a row atop his desk. Everything was muted yet enhanced by its subtle richness.

There were other details she didn't miss, either: a pair of costly jade earrings carelessly left behind in a Baccarat ashtray, for instance. She tried not to dwell on these facts, but instead looked out on the panorama beyond an immense piece of smoked glass covering one end of the room from floor to ceiling. Where in all the world, she wondered, could a more romantic view be seen? Orange lights outlined the bridges, and bright white lights ringed the wharfs and the shores of the bay. The hot fire clearly illuminated the room behind her, and its projected image shone against the glass. In the reflection, she watched Vic walk toward her. She turned and accepted the deep-green crystal tumbler he was holding. "This isn't coffee," she murmured.

"Not by a long shot! It's called *grappa,* and I guarantee it'll warm you faster than coffee."

Suspecting its potency, she took only a tiny sip. "This should be illegal!" A few seconds later, she got her breath back. She admired the way he drank the insidious liquid with ease, and she held up her glass in a symbolic salute. "I think your "humble home" is beautiful! I suppose this is where you lived with your parents, wasn't it?"

He nodded. "But at that time our whole apartment took up only a part of this room. Now I've taken over the entire floor, and I've put in a few improvements—a sauna, a space-age kitchen, knocked out walls, small things like that! I'm glad you like it." Balancing his glass, he sat down on the polished floor in front of the window. "Sit here by me. We can watch the ships gliding in and out of the bay together."

She gathered her long skirt beneath her legs and knelt down comfortably near him. His bandaged hand began to loosen the knotted black tie constricting his neck. As the fire crackled and sparked in a sudden updraft, she could clearly read the word etched on the gold band around his wrist. An emotion she would never have recognized as jealousy urged her to ask, "Does Carole Canova live here with you?"

"She visits once in a while."

She had to admire his diplomacy. What devilish whim had pushed her to ask such a prying question? But the subject didn't seem to bother him at all. In fact, he countered with a personal question of his own. "How long has Matt Moyer been in love with you?"

"Since before I was married. You're very perceptive, aren't you?"

"It wasn't hard to figure out. I saw how he looked at you."

"Did you also happen to notice that we're only close friends in spite of the fact that he's in love with me?"

"Yes . . . I saw the way you *didn't* look at him."

"You've reached a lot of conclusions about me, haven't you? Don't you think that's hasty and dangerous?"

"Not as dangerous or as wrong as some of the things you've been thinking about me." He leaned to rest on his arm, coming close to her. "Am I right, Laura?"

She couldn't bring herself to lie. "Yes, that's true. I almost hated you yesterday!"

"But that was yesterday . . ."

"And you promised we wouldn't talk about yesterday."

"We won't." He reached out a little and easily opened the tiny clasp that held her shoe together. Then he slipped the frail thing off her foot. With the back of his finger he lightly followed the curve of her instep. "Tell me about Frank Spandoni."

"He was a good man and a kind husband. . . ."

"He was more than old enough to be your father. Why did you marry him?"

"When my father became ill, he worried about leaving me alone with the responsibility of running the Winery. Frank Spandoni was his best friend and partner. . . ."

"You could have hired yourself a good company manager. Why did you *marry* him?"

"Because . . . he was . . . Because it was my father's last wish. . . ."

"I see." He didn't seem to be paying much attention to what she was whispering, however. By now he had removed her other shoe, and his palm was softly rubbing her slender ankle.

She sat very still and enjoyed the caress. When the pressure of his mouth replaced the feel of his hand, excitement, deep and involuntary, cut right through her. Her reaction was swift and arousing. Both hands sought the dark depths of his hair, and roughly entwined themselves in its thickness. And then her fingers slipped down to his open collar and stroked the dusky flesh between his throat and shoulder. Wherever she touched him, a fire sprang up to scorch her. She convulsively seized his shoulder beneath the shirt. His face turned away as his mouth began to follow an excruciating path along her leg, then her thigh, and then her hip. The ragged ebb and flow of his breathing and his almost brutal grip on her body told her exactly how fast and powerfully his raw desire had been triggered. As his full, hot mouth was forcing her lips apart, she whispered the truth, not an excuse, "I didn't come here to go to bed with you. . . ."

"I know. . . ." The words escaped in a throbbing murmur. "But you've been fighting a losing battle with yourself all night. . . ." He bent her backward until she found herself pinned between the hard floor and his hard body. "I think I lost the battle the moment I saw you. . . ."

"The moment I saw you." She had been dreading this forcefulness, fearing what it would awaken within herself. It was too late; what was now happening with Vic she had never known before. She didn't struggle to free herself. On the contrary, she raised herself to meet his mouth, coiling her arms tightly around his shoulders. Understanding that only a slow, sensual lingering would turn her on completely, he didn't hurry. His kiss burned, penetrating, demanding, satiating. The flimsy top of her dress was easily brushed aside. A stunning white heat suffused her silky breasts. "You went to bed with your husband obediently to satisfy him."

"Yes . . . no . . . I don't know. . . ."

"You never knew the difference between sex and pure pleasure with him . . . did you?"

"I . . . please, oh, please, don't . . ."

"Or with anybody else?"

"Vic!"

"Damn it, say it!" His ego demanded that she confess this terrible hunger aloud. But he knew, and knowing was enough to push him instantly beyond the point of all restraint. "You've never felt this . . . or this . . . or this . . . !"

A good, sweet fire spread downward from her lips as soon as his pulsating tongue moved to taste and lick and suck the small, rigid peak of her nipple. Then the hollows of her body began to moisten, and she vibrated and trembled in quick, short spasms, helpless against his touch. This, this was what she had needed so fiercely all along, and yet she had been resisting feeling it with Vic. She was in a dangerous game, but she didn't care. She couldn't stop him or herself now. The delightful agony he was inducing almost made her cry "Never, never like this, darling!" but she could only moan.

Suddenly enough to make her gasp, he pushed himself away. "Not here. Inside, in my bedroom." Dazed, unable to move, she watched him rip off his jacket and throw it aside. He bent down and ran his hands slowly from her breasts to her thighs. "You're so beautiful. That so-called husband of yours must have been crazy. . . ." He clutched her again and pulled her forward on her knees. She fell hard against him. "Tonight," he groaned, "I want only what you want, and I want you to be *selfish*, Laura. But tomorrow . . . !"

Tomorrow? Why did the thought of tomorrow stab like a streak of pain? What he was promising for tomorrow multiplied her fantasies almost to the brink of the unbearable.

He picked her up and carried her across the room. She spanned his strong back with her remaining strength, and with her other hand tore aside the thin shirt that frustrated her probing fingers. Now she could really feel his full, straining power. Tomorrow was too far away; only the next moments were real. But the truth kept nagging at her brain. The tighter she grasped him, the closer it came. Finally, she remembered. "I want you to love me tonight so much! But tomorrow . . . I can't stay with you until tomorrow . . ."

"Why not?" he demanded, breathless, his feverish mouth exploring every mysterious inch of her body. "Damn it, why not?"

Any number of reasons would be true, reasons that a little while ago had meant a great deal, but she knew that none of them mattered anymore. Never guessing the terrible mistake she was making, she chose the only important reason left. "Vic," she whispered, kissing the taut line of his clenched jaw, "I don't want to leave you, but I gave my word to present the Amici Award to this year's recipient. It's a very private, prestigious award," she continued, "and I was asked to represent my family at the luncheon. I was planning to write my little speech in the morning."

"The Amici Award?"

"Mm-m-m, yes . . ." She was floating, dreaming, and didn't notice the subtle change in his hold.

"And you were chosen to present the award?"

"It's traditional to have a member of a past recipient's family give the award each year."

"And, of course, your father . . ."

"Yes, he was honored with the award five years ago." His lips were still buried in her tumbled hair. She twisted to kiss him, but had to be content trailing her lips up and down his neck.

"Do you know who will be honored this year?"

"No, it's kept a great, big secret. Oh, the winner knows, I'm sure. Whoever he is, he has spent his life improving the art of winemaking. The committee wouldn't dare give it to someone who isn't the most respected and esteemed person in the industry. He has to be somebody . . . like my father, and he had to wait years and years! Let's not talk about it anymore, darling. What difference does it make to us who wins the Amici Award? That's tomorrow, and we have tonight . . . all of tonight. I only told you so you could understand why . . ."

"Yes, I understand a lot of things now."

He slowly let go of her. She slipped out of his arms, startled. "What's wrong?"

"Between us, you mean?" His face was dark, darker than ever, and his eyes were blank. "Too much is wrong, Laura."

Muddled, she had no idea how much anger he was suppressing. She thought he was teasing again. Of course! She had been stupidly explaining something he probably knew a little about, that was it! Maybe she didn't approve of his business methods, but he was somewhat involved in winemaking, wasn't he? "I forgot. I mean, you may be an outsider, but I'm sure somebody's told you about the Amici di Vino Award. This time I did sound like an awful snob, didn't I? Darling, I'm so sorry. . . ."

When he spoke, his voice was colder than ice. "Don't apologize. You're a D'Asti, remember? I'm sure no D'Asti has ever admitted to a mistake, especially to an *outsider.*" His stress on the last word was ugly. He turned away and walked over to a side table. He took a cigarette from a silver box, lit it, and then inhaled the smoke deeply without once glancing in her direction. "Get dressed."

The room was warm, almost hot, yet Laura trembled terribly. Finally, she grabbed her dress, pulled it on, smoothing back her hair as best she could. She would probably never forget the passion he had awakened, but her pride began to assert itself little by little. Finding her shoes and slipping them back on, she fought a surge of dizziness and waited a few moments to control herself. When she trusted herself to act rationally, she glanced at him. He still had his back to her. She crossed the room and faced him. "I'm not used to having a man turn his back on me."

He was staring into the fire, the shafts from its glow outlining the brutality in his features, the smoke of the cigarette curling up through the black hair that had felt so good when her fingers had caressed it. She reached up and snatched the cigarette from his lips. "Look at me! Tell me why you're treating me like this. I never intended to say anything that would upset you. It's true our lives have been very different, and . . . and I may be different from you, but Vic, I'm trying to understand you."

"Yeah, I said you were different, Laura. I didn't say you were better!" He lifted his jacket off the floor. "I'll take you home."

She was as stunned as if he had slapped her. It was revenge, pure and simple. He was seeking some kind of revenge. For what? She didn't know. Somehow she had attacked his male ego, and he was getting even in the worst way a man could hurt a woman.

He found the car keys. "Let's go."

"Don't bother!" She flung the cigarette into the fire, sending sparks and embers spewing out on the polished floor. Then she flew to pick up her shawl. "I wouldn't let you drive me home if I had to stop a stranger in the street and beg him to do me the favor!"

He got to the door before she could escape. "Stop acting like a spoiled, hysterical brat." He pulled her hand off the doorknob and crushed her fingers together in his fist. "I said I'd take you home—"

"Don't touch me!" Her voice was so full of loathing it threw him off guard for a second. She wrenched herself out of his grasp. "The only thing I'll ever want from you again is the sheer pleasure of watching you go straight to hell!"

He was left with the echo of her footsteps. The front door slammed shut with the finality of a curse.

CHAPTER FOUR

The Rolls purred along the streets with the grace of a gorgeous, self-indulgent black cat. Giorgio kept his eyes on the pedestrians and heard nothing of the conversation coming from the backseat. Not that it wasn't interesting, of course!

"You've been acting like a ghost all morning, and you look just as spooked. For crying out loud, luv, what happened last night?"

Laura wished Lucy would shut up. "I've told you over and over again, nothing happened last night." If her friend only knew the terrible irony of that remark!

"Don't hand me that jazz, Laura. I heard you moaning and crying all night."

"Don't be ridiculous. All you heard was the wind."

"Where did Vic take you?"

"To a little restaurant in North Beach owned by his cousin."

"Why did you come home in a cab? Did you run out on Vic because the place wasn't fancy enough for you?"

"What a nasty thing to say! As a matter of fact, the restaurant was excellent. I took a cab . . . because something went wrong with his car."

"I don't believe that for one minute! I know Vic, and he wouldn't allow anything to go berserk in that supercharged Italian torpedo he drives around."

"It's the truth. Oh, Lucy, please leave me alone!" If her head didn't stop throbbing, she knew she would scream. San Francisco had only two kinds of sky, foggy or bright blue. Today it was too bright. The sun beamed through the car windows, and it made her eyes burn.

Sleepless, haunted by Vic's sardonic image, she had stifled her sobs throughout the long night after arriving at Lucy's town house, hoping not to disturb Tina who was sharing the guest bedroom. But her sister had slept like a baby. Only Lucy had heard, even though her bedroom was on the other side of the elegant house. Her friend had sharp ears as well as a sharp mind; Lucy must have been up most of the night, too, puzzled and waiting for an explanation.

Ten times during the early morning Laura had sworn she would never get through the day, and she had nearly picked up the phone twice to call the Amici di Vino committee and say she was ill and couldn't attend the reception. But of all people, Giorgio had saved the day. Calmly and politely, he had ushered her onto the sunny patio and had served her strong coffee and fresh orange juice. Alone, drinking the hot coffee and watching the sun making patterns of light on the bridge, she swore she wouldn't give Vic Remo the satisfaction of wrecking her day! Finally, she even managed to put together a nice speech for the awards luncheon. Thank goodness, Lucy was still snoring after her all-night vigil, and Tina dashed in for only a second, gulped down a glass of juice, and then rushed out for a shopping spree that was sure to last all day. Her sister's brash comment about last night was short and to the point: "I don't blame you for skipping out of the opera with that Vic Remo, sis! I hope you had fun. He's unreal!"

Lucy was still harping on the night before as they drove to the reception. "Why didn't you tell me you knew Vic?"

"I don't know him. I met him the day before yesterday when he came to the Winery about some business."

Lucy leaped. "What business?"

"Nothing important. I don't even remember. Lucy, please!" She couldn't take much more. Today was going to be a disaster; she felt it in the pit of her stomach. The morning's resolve was deserting her rapidly, and she felt nauseated.

She almost jumped when Lucy reached over and took her hand, patting it warmly. Obviously, Lucy had decided to change tactics. "Maybe you didn't sleep all night and maybe you did, but anyway, you look very pretty this morning." Except for the torment in Laura's eyes, of course, but Lucy had the common sense not to mention that again.

"Thanks." Laura finally turned and smiled faintly at her friend. "This dress isn't too girlish, is it?" Taking extra care with her hair and makeup had helped her regain some of her calm. She still couldn't understand why she had chosen such a frivolous white dress, however.

"Naw! It's perfect. Look, luv, we're almost at the Palace of Fine Arts. Sure you don't want Giorgio to take you back to the house? I'll be glad to pinch-hit for you, and you can have the day to yourself. Maybe you could take a nice, long nap."

"No, thanks, I'll manage. Oh, Lucy," she muttered, "you're a wonderful friend, and I'm sorry I've been snapping your head off all morning."

"Hey, no big deal! What are friends for, right?" Her rather plain face turned motherly, and she gave Laura's hand a squeeze. "I'm going to say one more thing, and then I'll shut my mouth about you and Vic. Now, Laura, don't start protesting all over again! I wasn't born yesterday, you know. I want to tell you that contrary to what my readers may think of me—and I admit I've printed some dirty truths about this city's high society—a real heart does beat in this ample bosom of mine. Whatever's bothering the hell out of you, well, I'm ready to listen. Have you got that straight?"

"Yes, my dear Lucy. I've got that straight, and thanks."

"Good. Oh, we've arrived." Lucy had to take advantage of all the help Giorgio could offer before she got out of the limousine, but once on the sidewalk, she quickly regained her composure. "Laura, I want to see a big smile on that beautiful face of yours, and I want you to flash those gorgeous legs as much as possible." She fussed and tugged at the turquoise feathers sprouting all over her dumpy frame until she was sure everything looked perfect. "Now, come on! We make a glamorous pair, don't we? Let's go give some of those old geezers a heart attack!"

Arm in arm, Laura and Lucy laughingly rounded the lake where a corps of white swans was holding court. The Palace of Fine Arts formed a picturesque background for the graceful swans, and its Renaissance arcs and domes blended flawlessly with the sweep of the huge bay beyond. It was a magical scene, and Laura paused to look at it for a moment. An urgent voice broke into her reverie. "Lauretta! Miss Kaye!"

Coming up the slope at a brisk pace was one of the Amici di Vino's "old geezers." He extended his arms in warm greeting. A thoroughly delightful man Laura had known all her life, he was more than eighty years old, a world-renowned expert on wines, a millionaire, and an honorary president of the committee. "The ceremony is about to begin!"

"I'm sorry we're a little late, Signor Angelotti," Laura said, hugging the old man. "How are you?"

"Never better! Lauretta, my dear child, one of our new members is dying to meet you." He turned and signaled to a man walking in their direction. "May I introduce you to Ricardo Canova? Miss Kaye, why don't you let me escort you to your seat?" He tottered off with Lucy anchored firmly under his arm, warning over his frail shoulder that the luncheon was beginning.

If Laura hadn't been stung by hearing the name Ricardo Canova, she would have been amused at the spectacle of Lucy and Signor Angelotti together. Lucy was stumbling while attempting to look back to where Laura was standing.

When Laura finally turned her head, she encountered the coldest gray eyes she had ever seen and immediately visualized the diamonds around the haughty neck of Carole Canova. So this was Vic's boss. This was the man who wanted to steal her land and who was probably the guiding hand behind Vic's vicious business operations. Laura felt her dizziness returning.

"I wanted to meet you, Miss D'Asti, to tell you how much I admired your father."

"My father? Did you know him?" She hadn't expected

him to talk about her father. His choice of subject had been a stroke of genius; she had to admire his nerve.

"I met him a few times, but I was referring to his reputation."

Canova was slim, not too tall, and meticulously dressed. His silver hair gave the finishing touch to an appearance that would be called handsomely distinguished except for the coldness of his gray eyes, which sent a shiver up and down her spine. Laura could well imagine how easily he could dominate someone with that icy stare, so she wisely decided to stick to the truth. "My father earned his reputation by breaking his back in the fields to produce the finest wines in California. I intend to uphold his reputation, and I will continue to produce the finest wines for many years to come."

Everyone else was seated for the luncheon. He offered his arm. "An admirable if slightly misplaced mission for a woman."

She was forced to take his arm and choke back the strong retort that rose to her lips. Amid tables decorated with white roses, the Amici di Vino Awards Luncheon was being called to order. Laura walked beside Canova, loathing the touch of his hand. It filled her with the same coldness as his eyes. "Until a few days ago," she murmured just loudly enough for him to hear, "I knew your name only in connection with your banks." She looked straight ahead, acknowledging the smiles and greetings of people who were the very heart of the wine industry. Most were her friends. "How did you become a member of this honored wine society? Did you buy your way into this, too, Mr. Canova?"

He didn't answer, but he did look at her suddenly with new respect. "Let me take you to your table. I'm sure your seat is very near the head table. After all, where else would a D'Asti sit?"

She suffered his presence until she was seated alongside the long, rectangular head table, just as he had predicted. She dismissed him with a curt "Good-bye, Mr. Canova" and leaned over to talk to Lucy, a table away.

"Why did old man Canova want to meet you? It didn't have anything to do with that business deal Vic talked to you about, did it?"

"Sh-h-h. For goodness sake, Lucy, keep your voice down!"

"Okay, okay, but there's something creepy about that guy!"

"Those are exactly my sentiments." When Laura twisted back to face her table, she forced herself to make casual conversation with her neighbors and made an effort to pick at the epicurean foods that kept appearing before her during the long feast. She didn't feel dizzy or nauseated anymore; it was worse. She felt utterly numb. Somewhere near the end of the torturous meal, she realized she would never be able to speak in public this afternoon. She caught Signor Angelotti's eye and pleaded with him to find somebody to take her place. "I'm sorry, but I'm not feeling well. Would it be too much of a bother?"

"Not at all, my dear child," he said, patting her hand compassionately. "Will you be able to present the award to this year's recipient?"

"Yes, I can do that."

"I'm so glad! I'll make my remarks a little longer, that's what I'll do. Everybody will probably fall asleep," he jested, "but I'm sure they'll wake up when I announce who won the award! Oh, yes, this committee still has a few fresh tricks up its sleeve!"

Signor Angelotti tottered off, chortling over his secret. Laura took up her wineglass and drank for the first time today. Feeling suddenly better, she drank a little more of the wine. That was certainly a strange remark. Mulling over Signor Angelotti's mysterious words, she began to wonder who this year's recipient was anyway. She would know soon enough, however.

The tables had been cleared and coffee was being served from lovely antique silver urns when Signor Angelotti took up his position at the head table. His speech began with the usual remarks, and he went on to talk about the long and honored history of the Amici di Vino Awards. Laura half listened, and it wasn't until she raised the second cup of coffee to her lips that she heard him say something that captured her complete attention.

". . . Tradition is a marvelous thing, but the wine industry, as every other industry in the world today, must find men who look to the future, inventively using modern technology for the betterment of the industry and the product. Today we honor such a man, although he is new to our ranks. . . ."

No! It was impossible! There was no way Canova could have bribed the committee. All the money in the world couldn't have bought the Amici Award for Ricardo Canova. But the more Laura heard Signor Angelotti extolling the future and modern technology and dynamic salesmanship, the more she became convinced that Canova had accomplished the impossible.

". . . Because he had the imagination and foresight to envision a new market that had never been explored, our California wines are now being praised by the European connoisseur . . . ."

"Because he had the *gall* and the *money* to cheat small

growers out of their land!" she almost shouted. The coffee in her cup began to dance around as her hand suddenly started to shake. She quickly put the cup down on the saucer.

". . . The committee has chosen to break with the past and publicly recognize someone who will keep faith with our old traditions, but who will also mark the way toward greater opportunities for the California winegrower. With joy, I ask Miss Lauretta D'Asti to present this year's Amici di Vino Award in her illustrious father's memory . . ."

Oh, no, she wouldn't! Then and there, Laura decided she'd be damned if she would honor Canova with her own hands! They would just have to find somebody else!

". . . to a most worthy young man, Mr. Vic Remo!"

Someone kept shaking Laura; it had to be Lucy. "For God's sake, what's the matter with you, Laura? Stand up! Everybody's waiting for you!"

She managed to stand somehow. A few more steps and she had reached the head table. She even found the strength to give Signor Angelotti a tiny smile as she received the award from his hands. But she couldn't force herself to look at the faces in front of her for another second or so. When she finally did scan the crowd, she was even more shocked to see everyone applauding and looking so happy! The broadest smile of all radiated from the one face she thought could never show elation, Ricardo Canova's.

Vic must have been standing next to her for a while when Signor Angelotti reminded her, "Lauretta, my dear, we are waiting."

"Mr. Remo . . . I present you with the Amici Award." His dark hands reached to receive the beautiful scroll, and she saw the bandage was missing, although the marks of Bella's fangs looked quite angry. "On my behalf, and in my . . . my father's memory . . . I want, I mean, may I offer my congratulations."

"Thank you, Miss D'Asti." His voice was low but rich, and it contained a surprising ring of genuine emotion. "I'm especially honored receiving this award from you."

Her head snapped back, expecting to see a sarcastic smirk across his features. But she searched in vain. He looked sincere and so handsome!

She was saved from the frank appeal leaping out of those dusky eyes by the crowd of people gathering around the head table. Though trapped by the crush, she couldn't stand it anymore and found a way out. Once free of the Palace itself, she ran and didn't stop until she reached the edge of the lake. The swans didn't approve of the intrusion into their peaceful world and flipped water up in the air with their wings.

"Laura!"

"I don't want to look at your face!" She stood at the very brim of the bank and intently watched the swans.

"Why not?"

"After last night?"

"I know, Laura. I don't expect you to forgive me, but I only hope . . ."

"I don't care what you hope or want or do. And I certainly don't want to see you gloating!"

"I'm not gloating, I swear it. Laura, look at me."

"No."

"All right. But at least listen to me." Vic took a deep breath. "A month ago when I was told I had won the award, I was really surprised. Once the shock wore off, however, I realized it wasn't such a crazy idea. I've worked hard to improve the industry. . . ."

That remark brought her twirling around like a shot. "As far as I'm concerned, you've done *nothing*!"

He grabbed her shoulders and gave her a hard shake. "Do you know something? I'm getting a little fed up with your contempt!" His anger finally exploded. "Last night when you kept insisting only somebody who had sweat in the fields like your precious father was good enough to win the award, I could have . . ."

"You could have what?" He was bruising her horribly, but she didn't allow herself to flinch.

He suddenly realized how hard his fingers were digging into her soft flesh, and he let go, almost knocking her off balance. "You have a real talent for rubbing me raw, don't you?" he murmured, stepping away so that he wouldn't be tempted to grab her again. "Tell me, what is there about me that infuriates you so much?"

"You flatter yourself, Mr. Remo!"

"And you're a hypocrite, Miss D'Asti!" He stared her down and cut off her protests with a look that was beyond arrogance. "I've presented you with one hell of a problem since we've met, haven't I?"

"Problem? I don't know what you mean!"

"I think you know very well what I mean. While you've been looking down your aristocratic nose at me, you've also been begging me to pick you up and throw you on a bed and . . ."

She struck hard but blindly. He captured her hand in midair long before her palm came anywhere near his face and held it, crushing it unrelentingly. Completely absorbed in their struggle, neither heard Lucy's shriek. "Vic, stop it!" She screamed a second time before he freed

Laura's hand. "Have you gone completely off your rocker?" Lucy hissed, with murder in her eye. Her attention quickly turned toward Laura, who hadn't made a sound. "Did he hurt you, luv?"

Laura slowly moved her head from side to side. The flush that Vic's words had brought to her cheeks was now spreading downward as she saw that Ricardo Canova, among others, had witnessed the whole scene. "I'm all right! But, please, Lucy, let's get away from here!" She broke away from Lucy's hold and ran up to the street. Thank God, Giorgio had parked the car just ahead! As soon as Lucy huffed and puffed up the hill, blasting Vic with a few more choice words, Giorgio instantly brought the Rolls' motor to life, and the car shot down the street and out of sight.

The irritated swans circled around Vic's rigid form, cackling with malevolence. Frightened at the approach of a strong step, they scattered. "I haven't had a chance to really congratulate you, Vic. I'm very proud of you, my boy!"

Vic glanced down at the extended hand for a beat and finally clasped it. "Thanks, but you deserve the award as much as I do."

Canova's eyes showed warmth, if only for a moment. "Nonsense! I just had the common sense to recognize a real talent, that's all. I knew my investment in you would pay off." He peered at Vic and tried to remember the brash, poor youngster he had first known. Yes, indeed! All the money and all the effort had been well-spent. Vic Remo had turned out exactly as he had planned. However, there was a point or two that had to be clarified. "I would like the D'Asti contract signed and delivered as soon as possible." If he knew Vic, a small threat would only spur him to act faster. "Since you and Laura D'Asti seem to have some bad blood between you, I'm relieving you of this particular assignment."

"No!" There were many reasons why Vic's ego wouldn't let him accept defeat when it came to the D'Asti deal. "I started the negotiations and I'll finish them. But, damn it! Why didn't you tell me the truth about Laura? I went out to Sonoma expecting to find a helpless old hag, and instead I found a beautiful . . . I mean, she's young and so . . ."

"It was your job to find out that information, not mine," Canova murmured. Vic had just told him everything he needed to know about this business. Was it possible that Vic had finally met his match in Laura D'Asti? She was beautiful, but she was strong-willed, too. Sex and business mixed well sometimes, but love and business, never. Still, Vic deserved another chance. "Handle it any way you want then, but I want that contract signed within seventy-two hours. Now let's forget about that and talk about something else." Since he didn't know how to approach the subject, he decided to be blunt. "Carole spent last night crying her eyes out. What happened between the two of you?"

"That's none of your business." Vic could feel himself getting ready to explode again. He didn't want to talk about Carole, especially not with her doting father. "Carole's a big, bright girl with a trail of divorced corpses behind her. I wouldn't worry, Canova. She can take care of herself."

"She's my daughter, and I love her." The expression in his cold eyes never varied. "She thinks she's in love with you."

"Then she's making a big mistake, because I haven't promised her anything."

"That's not how she sees it. . . ."

"Then she's lying to herself, and she's also lying to you. Look, Canova, I told you I don't want to discuss this," he snapped, turning to walk away.

Canova caught him by the arm. "I want her to be happy."

"Then stay out of her life." He shook off Canova's hard grip. "As for me, all you have to know is I'll get you that D'Asti land."

CHAPTER FIVE

Tina watched carefully as her sister walked back and forth in the sunny bedroom, intently sorting out clothes from a suitcase. Complaining of a terrible headache, Laura had left all the driving to Tina on yesterday's dash home from San Francisco, and they had arrived at the Winery late. Tina had flopped down on her bed immediately and fallen asleep. Obviously, so had Laura, because she was only now unpacking. "I'm sorry you got so sick at the Amici luncheon, Laura. Do you feel better this morning?"

Laura stopped to ponder her sister's question, the white shawl she had worn to the opera slipping through her fingers. "Yes, much better, thanks, honey."

She didn't look better. In fact, she looked worse, Tina thought, stretching out on her belly across Laura's bed.

Bella, whom Laura had ignored all morning, raised herself off her haunches and sashayed over to muzzle Tina's drooping hand, begging for affection from somebody. While absentmindedly rubbing the sad creature's ears, Tina continued to watch Laura's nervous movements. It was a hot morning, and it promised to be an even hotter day. Both women had opted to wear as little as possible. Tina had thrown on a bikini bra and briefs, but Laura was still clad in the shortest of nighties, which clung damply to her breasts and hips.

Regardless of the dark smudges under her eyes, Laura was still the loveliest woman she had ever seen, Tina decided. She desperately wished that whatever demons were pecking away at Laura's soul would go away forever! Tina surmised that something terrible must have happened at the luncheon yesterday. When she had returned from shopping expecting to find an empty town house, she had found instead Lucy looking uptight and Laura positively green. Giorgio had already stashed their luggage in the Winery's ancient station wagon, and Laura insisted they begin the long trek back home immediately. Tina had been able to steal only a second alone with Lucy, and all she got out of her was some gibberish that sounded like, "That Vic Remo! I'll kill him if I ever get my mitts on him!"

Vic Remo again. Although Laura's dark moods had begun before this Mr. Remo had stepped into her life, Tina was sure that that gorgeous man had been the catalyst of her sister's present near-collapse. Virtually on pins and needles over the mystery surrounding Vic Remo, Tina tried to coax some information out of Laura as diplomatically as possible. "It would have been great to have spent a few more days in the city, wouldn't it? If you hadn't gotten sick, I mean."

Laura folded a few more articles of clothing and put them in the top drawer of her dresser. Keeping her back to Tina, she nodded and then murmured, "I promised to take you to lunch. I'm so sorry we never made it."

"Oh, that's okay," Tina quickly assured her, wondering how she could maneuver the conversation around to Vic Remo. "We'll try some other time soon. You haven't told me much about the luncheon. Any *interesting* people?"

"Yes, of course. It was nice to see a lot of Papa's friends again."

That wasn't what Tina wanted to hear. "Any, well . . . new faces?"

"Why did you ask that?" Laura turned and looked cautiously at her sister.

"I was wondering if Vic Remo was there. I thought I heard Lucy mention his name yesterday." Tina wasn't called pert for nothing!

"Yes, he was there."

The note of finality in Laura's voice wrenched Tina's heart. Not wishing to cause Laura any more pain, she asked instead, "Well, aren't you going to tell me who won the Amici Award?"

Laura took a deep breath. She could try to continue this charade as casually as possible, or she could let herself go to pieces, slipping into the hysteria she had been fighting all morning. But a closer look at Tina's bright, pretty face suddenly made it plain that she had a third choice—she could tell Tina the truth in so far as Vic Remo and the Winery and Ricardo Canova were concerned. After all, why not? Tina was a D'Asti, and the Winery was her legacy, too. Laura stopped unpacking, and with a heartfelt sigh of relief she sat down on the bed and faced her not-so-little sister. "Vic Remo won the Amici Award . . . ."

"But," Tina cried, really surprised, "that's impossible! What does he have to do with wines?"

Fondly grasping Tina's hands, Laura explained Canova's plot to acquire prime vineyards in Sonoma, and she didn't stint on the mercenary reasons Vic was involved in the schemes, either. But she had explained herself into a corner. "Our Winery's in trouble, financial trouble. Oh, it's nothing new, really, and it's nothing I want you to worry about. When Papa got sick . . . well, that's when the problem started."

"Is that why you married Frank Spandoni?" Tina gave Laura's hand a squeeze. She wanted to understand her sister and all her problems better.

"Yes, Papa thought Frank could pull the Winery out of its difficulties, but he couldn't. Anyway," Laura murmured, "he was killed before he really had a chance to try to save the Winery."

"Laura, do you miss him?"

"Frank? What a silly thing to ask! Of course, I miss him."

"I mean do you miss him as a husband?"

Laura was shaken, not because she was afraid to answer Tina's question but because Tina had been wise enough to ask it. She suddenly realized that Tina probably had guessed the real conflict between Vic Remo and herself. Laura allowed herself a smile. So this was the baby sister she had been protecting!

"Truthfully, Tina . . ." She broke off as Tina's eyes narrowed in warning. Lithely Tina jumped off the bed and rushed noiselessly to the door. She flung the door open and then dashed out into the large hallway that ran the entire length of the mansion. In a moment, the door slammed shut, and Tina was back in Laura's bedroom, looking furious.

"What was it?" Everything had happened so fast that Laura still sat on the bed.

"Listen, Laura," Tina muttered, keeping her voice low, "I'm about to offer you some advice! I have a few good ideas how we can cut corners and save money and maybe save the Winery, but the first thing you must do is to throw out that selfish, freeloading, sneaky old witch!"

"Donna Evangelina?"

"Who else?" Tina jumped back on the bed. She was quickly followed by Bella, who was beginning to like all the excitement. "I just caught a glimpse of her awful black dress as she went scooting into her room. This isn't the first time I've caught her eavesdropping and snooping, either! Oh, sis, why don't you send that pious old hypocrite back to Italy where she belongs? You treat her like a queen, and yet she hates you!"

"I can't turn her out of my house," Laura said, feeling the stab of an old guilt. "She is Frank's mother, and as long as she lives she'll be my responsibility and she'll be treated with respect." She softened the lecture by giving Tina a hug. "Thanks for the advice, anyway. Now, what about telling me some of those good ideas you have that might save the Winery?"

"I could postpone graduation for another year. Meanwhile, I could find a job and help you a little bit."

"Absolutely not!" Bella, forbidden to frolic on the furniture, jumped off the bed with a loud yip at Laura's sharp cry. "You must finish college, and then you'll be able to help me much more, don't you understand?"

"I suppose you're right. But why can't I help Matt now? He'll need an assistant as soon as the wine ages, and that's always very costly. I can do the job! I'm turning into a very good enologist, you know."

Laura took a moment to think that over. "Now, there you've come up with a darned good idea! Only I don't want this work to interfere with your studies."

"Don't worry, it won't. In fact, I'll probably get extra-work credit for it at the university. Ah, this is great! I'll be helping you and the Winery, and I'll be working with Matt!"

As Laura watched Tina glow at the very thought of working side by side with Matt Moyer, she decided she should once and for all rub out the only sore spot that had ever existed between them. Neither of them ever mentioned it, yet it was there. "Tina, I want to tell you something very important." Again she had the strange feeling that the girl knew exactly what she was about to say. "Matt and I have always been just good friends."

"But he's always been in love with you, Laura."

"No, he hasn't." She lovingly smoothed Tina's hair away from her face. "He'll know the difference when he finds somebody who will really love him . . . somebody like you."

"Ah, Laura, I always thought . . ."

The next few minutes were spent in stifling sniffles and giving in to silly giggles. Suddenly the phone rang, and Laura became nervous again. "I don't want to talk to anyone."

Tina answered, but Laura could easily hear Lucy Kaye's strident voice demanding to speak to Laura. She hesitated but finally took the phone from Tina's hand. After all, she really owed her kind friend some explanation for her bizarre behavior.

"Hello, Lucy. Did you get back to Sonoma this morning . . . ?"

* * *

As she drove toward the town square, Laura was happy she had given in to Lucy's pleas to meet for lunch at the famous old Vallejo House. It was Sonoma's favorite place to relax, enjoy good food, and talk. She drove slowly around the four sides of the old plaza, looking in vain for a parking spot. There were throngs of people everywhere, almost more than the small shops and restaurants could handle. As Laura started to round the plaza again, a van pulled away and Laura took the spot immediately.

The Vallejo House was across the park, but Laura didn't mind the hike. The day was warm, dry, and glorious. Crisscrossing the road, she cut through the familiar plaza, with its lush lawns, ponds, and lines of plane trees marking the main walks. She smiled as usual at the ugliness of the bronze monument erected to the Bear Flag Republic by the well-meaning Native Daughters of the Golden West. She much preferred the plain honesty of City Hall, which stood in the center of the plaza. Built of stone from the nearby Sonoma Mountain, the building's central tower housed a large bronze clock, a gift from Laura's father that the family maintained in perfect working condition.

The sight of the clock reminded Laura that the delicate instrument would soon need its annual overhaul. More money! Coming out of the plaza's gardens, she glanced at a large redwood structure she must have passed a dozen times, but this time its opulent facade seemed to smirk back at her. It was the Canova Bank. This was only one of many branches throughout California, of course. The main bank was headquartered in a magnificent complex in San Francisco. Did Vic have his offices in that complex? she wondered.

Turning her face abruptly, she walked through the

grand old park behind City Hall, taking off her sandals so that her feet could sink into the cushiony grass. She hadn't gone far when the one subject she had been trying to avoid thinking about suddenly overwhelmed her. Vic Remo! She had fled his apartment that night more humiliated than she had ever been in her life. But the next day—yesterday—she had been forced to smile and be civil, further humiliating herself by presenting him with the Amici Award. She strolled on a little faster now, physically propelled by the rush of emotion that engulfed her as she remembered his crude insinuation afterward. What a joke that had been! *He* had planned that cozy little seduction, not she, and his deceitful scheme had turned against *him!* For a while, all during the long night after she had left his apartment, she had felt remorse for whatever it was she had said that had hurt him so badly. Not knowing the reason for his sudden coldness, she had imagined all sorts of causes, none very flattering to herself! But yesterday everything had been clarified. Now she knew exactly how base he could be. Had Canova's evil genius hatched the plan to bewitch her out of her lands? Or had both men gotten their kicks planning it together? Or had Vic merely resorted to his reliable technique to get what he wanted? Well, he had certainly struck out this time!

Elated by the thought of how frustrated he must be feeling, Laura came to the edge of the park and saw Lucy waving to her from the patio of the Vallejo House. It never occurred to her that she was completely ignoring her own hunger for him and the possibility that part of his insulting accusation could be true.

"You're late, Laura! I was beginning to think you weren't coming." Lucy looked worried, exasperated, and limp from the heat. Her costume was rather sedate, but she spoiled the modest effect by sporting a large cowboy hat atop her head, complete with garish feathered band. "What took you so long, luv?"

"I was strolling through the park, it was so cool and quiet. I'm sorry you've been out here in this heat waiting for me." Laura smiled foolishly at the shoes still clutched in her hands. She quickly slipped them on.

"I'm glad you could relax for a few minutes." Lucy beamed. "You look like a lovely young gypsy, with that pretty blue peasant skirt and blouse."

"I just couldn't bear to wear anything more formal in this heat." Laura laughed and smoothed down the long flared skirt and straightened the low-cut edge of the thin blouse.

They walked slowly along the patio, falling under the spell of the verdant setting that surrounded the restaurant. A restored California colonial long house, the historic Vallejo home featured Napa-Sonoma's most unique garden. The basic plan of the grounds had been inspired by the mystical gardens of the Alhambra, and the delightful array of flora included olives, grapefruits, pomegranates, and lemons identical to those found in the summer palace of the Moorish caliphs in Granada, Spain. General Mariano Guadalupe Vallejo, the powerful Comandante de Alta California had built this great *estancia* only twenty years before the first D'Asti had come to Sonoma to grow grapes. The general had named his home Lachryma Montis, the "tear of the mountain," because of a crystal-clear creek that bubbled and tumbled its way through the grounds. That playful creek still cooled the gardens before disappearing underground in a stunning replica of the famous Lion's Fountain in the courtyard of the Alhambra.

Laura halted by the fountain and let her fingers drift

under the sheet of water pouring from the mouth of one of the four massive stone lions. She had loved this spot ever since she had been a child. She frequently had accompanied her family to dinner at the invitation of the descendants of the Vallejos, who then still owned the property. She looked around with a contented sigh at the estate, now a designated State Historical Site. "Lucy, you and your volunteers have done a wonderful job with this place."

"It's been a labor of love, believe me." Lucy squinted, took off her hat, and gave her tousled hair a shake. The *estancia* had been in very sad condition when she had spearheaded the drive to restore it, and she had sunk a lot of her own money into the project. She had a special love for the place, too. Her own newspaper's offices were situated in what had been the old carriage house. "But it was your charity parties at the Winery that really pulled in the money," Lucy reminded Laura. "Say, when are you going to let me put on another charity luncheon there?"

Laura didn't feel that she could pull herself together for a social bash, no matter how worthy the cause. "Soon," she hedged.

Lucy didn't press the point. "I'm hungry as a bear. Come on, luv, let's eat." She plopped the horrible cowboy hat back on her head.

Reaching the lunch pavilion, several of the gardeners and staff waved at Lucy and Laura. They were seated at a choice table under an ornamental fig tree, and a perky little waitress in a long calico dress immediately came over to take their order. "Hello, Miss Kaye! Why, Miss D'Asti, we haven't seen you in a while. Welcome back!"

"Thanks, Suzie." Laura didn't have to study the menu;

she knew it by heart. "I think I'll have the California salad—"

"Make that two," Lucy interrupted, shrugging and pointing to her broad waistline. "I hate rabbit food, but I've decided to go on a diet."

Laura and Suzie tried hard not to laugh, but Suzie finally couldn't help giggling. "Oh, Miss Kaye, if you're on a diet, you don't want a salad that's made of creamy chicken chunks garnished with roasted sesame seeds and great, yummy wedges of avocado, do you?"

"Sure, I do, and I want extra helpings of avocado. I may be on a diet, but I don't want to starve to death!"

Suzie went away with their order, still giggling, and Laura couldn't postpone the inevitable any longer. "My friend, I owe you an explanation, I think."

"You don't owe me anything." Lucy leaned back in her chair. The play of sunlight on her plain features seemed to bring out something pretty in her face, especially after she removed that ridiculous cowboy headgear. "However, I'm ready to listen to anything you feel like telling me."

Laura thought this over for a moment. Why not? She couldn't go on keeping all this inside herself much longer! "The Winery is still in deep trouble . . ."

"And my offer to help you with some bucks still stands."

"And my answer is still no! But thanks again, Lucy. I only brought up the subject because Ricardo Canova found out about my Winery's deficit, and that's why he sent Vic Remo out to see me the other day. Canova desperately wants my land, and he won't be satisfied until he gets it."

"Look, Laura, maybe it's not such a bad idea, selling Canova your land, I mean."

"Are you crazy . . ." She was about to say much more, but Suzie returned with their food. The salads were astounding and had to be commented on and praised. Also, Suzie had brought a bottle of D'Asti prime white wine to the table in homage to Laura, and the thoughtful girl had to be thanked for her lovely gesture. As soon as Suzie left, however, Laura hissed, "What do you mean, sell Canova my land?"

"Just that. Listen to me for a moment. Canova's been buying quite a few wineries, and he's always paid absolutely top price. He continues to operate the wineries as first-class operations, and the ex-owners can have a marvelous time spending all that lovely loot. So, what's wrong with getting rid of that outdated vineyard? You're still young and beautiful and could have oodles of Canova's money to throw around for the rest of your life! What's the matter with you, do you like suffering?"

"I thought you would understand!" Laura couldn't believe it. "I won't sell my Winery to Canova! I hate him—and I hate Vic Remo, too!"

"So that's it," Lucy said, squinting and pouring some of the wine. "You hate Canova, so that makes you hate Vic also."

Laura took the glass and drank. "Mr. Remo has earned my loathing quite on his own merits."

"Why? Did he make a healthy, red-blooded sexual move that you mistook as a devious way to rob you of your land?"

"I didn't mistake anything. That's exactly what he did."

"Then you've got Vic Remo all wrong. He makes his business deals at his office, not in his bedroom."

Laura fiddled with her salad and then threw her fork

down in disgust. "What makes you such an authority on Vic? Why are you always defending him?"

"First, because I've known him since he was a kid, and second, because he's one of the few people in this world I really love."

Laura hadn't expected such an answer. She peered at Lucy. Her friend looked serious and sincere. "Then I'm sorry for the things I've been saying about him. Let's talk about something else." She gave up on the salad altogether and poured herself some more wine. It was vintage D'Asti, worth a battle with Vic or anybody else!

"No, let's talk about Vic," Lucy insisted, pushing aside the hated rabbit food and joining Laura in another drink. "When I was young and stupid, I ran away from my wealthy home and naturally decided that some suffering would help me find myself. I took a cold flat in North Beach in San Francisco and suffered for a year. Oh, I did the whole bit, I froze, I starved, I became infested with fleas—and I didn't prove a damned thing! I even became a vegetarian, so help me!" She glared at the plate heaped with avocado and gave it another vicious shove across the table. "The only good thing that came out of my idiotic experiment was that I always bought my damned veggies at the Remo's market. I got to know those beautiful people real well. Mama and Papa Remo really worshipped Vic, and that little kid thought the world of his parents. Nothing mushy, just plain love. He built that gorgeous body of his hauling crates around that store since he was eight years old, but he never seemed to resent the hard work. Oh, sure, he's rich now, but he still works hard for his money. He hasn't changed much since those days—changed inside, I mean—and we've remained good friends."

"Sometimes, even a good friend can't tell if a person has changed . . . ."

"With Vic, it's easy." Lucy laughed. "Forget the icy exterior; inside, he's all Sicilian—generous, joyful, passionate." Then she shrewdly struck at the heart of Laura's problem. "I can't blame you for flipping over the guy in spite of the fact that a bit of the snob in you doesn't think he's good enough for a D'Asti!" She quickly waved away Laura's outraged protest. "Neither you nor Vic have fooled me, luv. You've gotten under his skin, too, and you're doing funny things to his ego. Have you forgotten that I saw that emotional scene you both pulled over by the ducky-wucky pond yesterday?" She also conveniently left out the detail that she could have bopped Vic for losing his cool yesterday. This little gal needed lots of tender loving care, not brute force. But Lucy had forgiven Vic, and she had great faith in him!

Laura, meanwhile, was thinking furiously. This girl-to-girl talk wasn't turning out right. Backed against the wall, she stalled for time by pouring some more wine. "I'm not a snob, but I was taught to respect certain values."

"That's a poor excuse for being afraid to admit you're physically attracted to somebody, or that you're starting to fall in love with him."

"Lucy, for goodness sake, that's not what I'm talking about!"

"Oh, yes, it is, and don't you kid yourself!" Lucy was gazing at Laura with pity, but there was a great deal of understanding, too. "As crazy as this sounds, you and I have a lot in common." She chuckled at Laura's puzzlement. "Okay, so you were born beautiful and I was born ugly, but we're both Sonoma gals with roots that go back to the Spanish Republic. We were both brought up to buckle under family authority. Because I felt guilty as hell about my year of bohemian freedom, I gave in to my father's bullying and married somebody my mommy and daddy had hand-picked for me."

This really startled Laura. "I never knew you were married. Somehow," she confessed, "I've never thought of you as the marrying type. You're too independent."

"You're right, I'm not the marrying type. I found that out only a few days after the wedding."

"What happened to your husband?"

"My husband was a nice guy who had been pressured by *his* family to marry me. He was a jerk. No, I didn't divorce him; I merely misplaced him somewhere in Africa, where we had gone on our so-called honeymoon. I handed him a blank check and turned him loose. He was as glad to get rid of me as I was to get rid of him! I never saw him again, and years later I had the marriage annulled. I'm glad I had the guts to call it quits right at the beginning. It would have been a rotten marriage!"

Laura bristled. "That's where you and I differ. My marriage wasn't rotten."

"If it helps your pride to say that, then I'll accept it."

The two women stared at each other in the quiet of the garden. Laura's eyes fell first. "Perhaps if you had given your marriage more of a chance," Laura murmured, trying to hide her own unhappiness, "you wouldn't be spending all these years alone."

"I'm not alone."

"You're not . . . What do you mean?"

Lucy debated whether or not to confide in this girl. She wasn't afraid of Laura's disapproval, nor would she be hurt by it. Only Laura could be hurt by the loss of their friendship. She decided to take the chance. "I met somebody I could really love about ten years ago. A bit late in life, but not *too* late. I thumbed my nose at everybody, and I took the gamble. I'm glad I did because Giorgio and I have been very happy ever since."

Laura knew she had heard wrong. "Giorgio? He's your chauffeur, Lucy, he's your chauffeur!"

"That's right. I've tried to make an honest man of him, but he won't marry me. He likes everything the way it is. I suppose you could say he's independent, too." Lucy sadly shook her head. "You're shocked."

"No."

"Yes, you are. It's a pity that you're shocked for all the wrong reasons, however."

"I'm not shocked! I'm very surprised, that's all."

Suzie had hesitated to intrude on the tense conversation, but she quickly ran up with the bill when the older woman signaled to her. Suzie loved serving Lucy Kaye, the newspaperwoman regularly left a very large tip, and she was such a scream!

When Suzie scampered away with a glowing smile and a fistful of money, Lucy looked at Laura's expressionless face and then stood up with a sigh. "Newspapers don't print themselves, so I guess I'd better get back to work."

"Lucy!" Laura jumped out of her seat and stood, wavering and miserable, a short distance from her best friend. "Please tell me the truth. Do you think Vic deserved to win the Amici Award?"

"You're damned right, I do!"

"You're not just saying that because you like him?"

"Look, luv, I was as stunned as you were when old Angelotti announced Vic the winner, but I quickly realized he had really earned the award. Believe me, I was twice as hard on Vic because he's my friend. Come on, be fair! Times have changed, and the old ways are not always the best ways, you know."

Laura was ready to concede that point, but another possibility still nagged at her. "Then you don't think Canova's money could have persuaded the Amici committee to vote for Vic?"

"Be realistic!" Lucy bellowed, exasperated. "All those old geezers are multi-millionaires. They don't need Canova's money. And they are all men of the highest moral caliber. Tell me," Lucy asked, hitting the nail right on the head, "do you think your father could have been bribed?"

Laura put her hands up to her eyes, thoroughly confused and upset. "Oh, Lucy! Maybe I've been wrong!" She threw herself into Lucy's arms, hugging her fiercely without any explanation.

For once, Matt Moyer looked very determined. He had been waiting for Laura to return from Sonoma, and he quickly opened the car door as she stopped by the arbor. "Laura, I want to talk to you."

She knew why. The aging wine had reached a critical stage. Her heart sank, but she tried to look unconcerned nevertheless. "It's so hot. Why don't we go into the house and get something cold to drink, Matt?" She darted toward the mansion, hoping to postpone the inevitable as long as possible. "We might as well make ourselves comfortable while we talk about unpleasant things, right?"

"Yes, thanks. Perhaps you're right." His eyes became opaque behind his sandy glasses, but the grimness around his mouth remained unchanged. "A few more wasted minutes won't make any difference, I suppose."

Harshness was not something she expected from Matt, but she knew he was under a great deal of pressure. Pressure! Lately, every action, every detail, brought more pressure bearing down on her shoulders, too. She was drained from this afternoon's encounter with Lucy. She wanted to lock herself in her bedroom and not think about anything.

Tina's bright and cheery "Hello!" snapped her out of her reverie. "I thought you were returning to the university this afternoon?"

Tina put the full tray of frosted espresso glasses down on the shaded veranda table with a proud tilt to her head. "I'm supposed to help Matt, remember, sis? I called the university this morning after you left to have lunch with Lucy, and I told my professor about our plan. He thought it was a super idea, so I don't have to attend lectures until next week." She looked so happy. "Now, stop acting like a grouch and come and have some iced coffee! You too, Matt."

He looked completely confused. "Help *me*, Tina? Help me with what?"

Tina's gaze shifted to Laura, and Laura got the hint. "I'll explain everything in a minute, Matt. Meanwhile, why don't you sit down." She suspected her sister had been planning this little party all afternoon. The girl's face was a study in rapture every time she glanced at Matt. Laura wanted to help this unorthodox courtship as much as possible.

Matt sat down and smiled vaguely at Tina when she handed him the cold glass of creamy espresso. "Help me with what?" he persisted.

"Tina and I hatched this plan. See what you think of it, Matt." Laura told him of Tina's idea to help him with the processing of the aging wine. When she had finished, both sisters waited for his reaction.

"It's a very good idea," he conceded, thinking it over

carefully. He smiled broadly at Tina, but then he began to shake his head. "But we may not have any wine to process!"

"Is it that critical?" Laura whispered.

"Yes. I would say that if I keep the wine in those casks sleeping for more than seventy-two hours, we're going to lose the whole batch."

"And I will lose the Winery," Laura thought. The distinct possibility of that happening hit her fully for the first time. Everything would be lost along with the land, and all her sacrifices wouldn't amount to a grain of salt. She couldn't bear it. Vic had been right when he had said that.

"Thanks for thinking I can be of some help to you," Tina said, a little miffed that Matt had slurred over her offer of assistance so casually. "I've really learned the craft, you know."

"I'm sure you have, Tina," he hastened to apologize, "and I'll like working with you, only . . ." He was too frustrated to finish.

"Don't be so gloomy, you two! There are many new methods we could try before we give up," Tina declared. "How about freezing the wine? Have you thought about that?"

"Too expensive and too unpredictable," he argued immediately.

"We can experiment with other methods, can't we? What have we got to lose!"

Tina and Matt became engrossed in a heated debate about the pros and cons of various delaying techniques. Laura, meanwhile, stirred the frothy liquid in her glass and said nothing. She was curiously numb; it took all her energy just to hold up her glass. No amount of reason or theory would save the wine, she knew, and she listened to the babble of technical terms being flung between Tina and Matt with growing nervousness. Finally, she couldn't stand it anymore. "Why don't you take Tina to dinner or somewhere for a drink," she said to Matt suddenly. "There's nothing more that can be done tonight, and both of you can use a break. We can begin testing the wine again early in the morning. Right now, we're all too tired to think straight." Go! Just please go away!

Matt's mild face looked shocked. "I can't leave now! I plan to spend the rest of the night taking samples from those casks. . . ."

"Oh, no, you're not!" Tina said, resolved to take matters into her own hands as far as Matt was concerned. Laura had just handed her a wonderful opportunity, and she was about to take full advantage of the situation. "Laura's the boss, and she has the last word, remember? You may take me out to dinner, and we can finish our talk while we relax a little. Matt, don't be so stubborn!"

Trapped between two strong temperaments, Matt gave in. "All right, all right! Maybe things will look better in the morning, who knows? Tina and I might just figure out something tonight to save the wine," he told Laura, not sounding the least bit convinced himself. He cleared his throat shyly. "I would very much like to take you to dinner, Tina." He quickly remembered his manners. "Laura, why don't you come with us?"

She didn't need Tina's eloquent stare to make up her mind. "No, thanks." The sun was setting, and dusk was descending swiftly. The darkest of nights loomed ahead, and she wanted to face it alone. "I'll skip dinner tonight and get some sleep."

"You could use some rest," Tina agreed, "and you won't have to worry about the old witch, oops! I mean

Donna Evangelina. She has one of her simply excrutiating headaches. I took a tray of her favorite goodies up to her room, so she won't be down for dinner."

"That was very kind, Tina." Laura mumbled a few more words at the pair, and then she turned and walked into the shadows of the silent house. Her footsteps echoed distinctly as she crossed the large entryway that led to the stairs. She forced herself to walk more softly and lightly. She hurried by Donna Evangelina's room at the top of the stairs and almost ran to her own bedroom at the end of the long hallway. Rushing into her room, Laura pushed the door shut, carefully turned the lock, and then remained leaning against the door for support. Usually so airy, the room was hot. She quickly opened all the windows and breathed in what little air managed to filter into the space around her. The night breezes, usually cool and comfortable, were dense and torrid.

Laura was beginning to feel light-headed. Stripping off the light skirt and blouse, she listlessly moved toward the bathroom, and without even bothering to turn on the lights she stepped into the shower. The torrent of water shot out barely lukewarm. Ordinarily, she would have adjusted it to a warmer setting, but this time she relished the coolness on her skin. Twisting and swaying so that the soothing spray could reach every part of her body, she plunged her hands into the thickness of her hair, bending her head forward to catch the full flow of the water. How good it felt! The strain of the day began to leave her taut limbs as she rubbed her favorite creamy liquid soap all over herself. She then repeated the same ritual on her long hair, washing it with a spicy, tangy lemon shampoo.

The bath towel had fallen carelessly to the floor, and Laura had just picked up her hairbrush when she heard the light tapping on the bedroom door. It was Tina, of course, saying that she had changed her clothes and would be leaving with Matt in a second. Laura didn't answer, hoping her sister would think she was asleep. She couldn't help it; she didn't want to speak to anyone. The harmless deception worked, and Tina could be heard running down the stairs.

The room was still swathed in darkness. Laura could approach the window without being seen by anyone standing below on the lawn. Tina's feet fairly flew over the front steps as she met Matt. They got into his car and quickly disappeared from Laura's view.

Good luck, sis! Laura turned away from the window smiling to herself and flicked on a small lamp on her night table. The room hadn't cooled much, so she decided to dress and walk outside for a while. Putting on a light silk shirt with matching white ducks and the slenderest of sandals, she brushed her hair until it glistened like copper, turned out the light, and left the bedroom.

Instead of leaving the house as she had planned, Laura turned to climb the sharply tilted stairwell that led to the roof of the mansion. She didn't know what had brought her to this spot, but she walked over to the very edge of the ornate guard that circled the very top of the house. She was very happy she wasn't bothered by heights; if she had reached behind her, she could actually have touched the uppermost cupola of the beautiful old mansion.

The night was glorious. Nothing moved. The air was stunningly still, and the full moon shed such a luminous light that objects in the far distance were clearly visible. Laura could see the peaks of Sonoma's buildings and the bell tower of the Vallejo House. Her thoughts immediately returned to Lucy's astounding confession. Inconceivable, yet true: Giorgio had been Lucy's lover for years! "Well," Laura told herself, brushing her heavy hair away from her skin, "why not?" Lucy was obviously very happy with the relationship, and Giorgio certainly seemed content and satisfied, so why not!

Her eyes were caught by the flare from a bonfire carefully set by some of the Winery's workers, preparing for a merry *festante* of some sort. The sweet strains of a mandolin reached her, a traditional Neapolitan love song. She looked beyond to her vineyards, which spread out from the house in all directions. The precious vines looked like hundreds of miniature soldiers in the moonlight, all lined up in perfect marching order, seemingly stretching across the fertile earth to infinity.

Laura shivered in spite of the heat. She was responsible for all that land, and the awesome responsibility was crushing her. She laughed at the irony of the moment. Alone, she was standing on the widow's walk, gazing out on a world teeming with life. Mocking her self-pity, she whirled around and concentrated on the majesty of Sonoma Mountain, which loomed over her property and all the rest of the Valley of the Moon. As a youngster she had scampered up and down its slopes, happily and carelessly exploring the mountain's mysteries until the day she had discovered the ancient cemetery. She could still remember how frightened she had become, finding the name D'Asti engraved just as frequently as the legendary name Vallejo on the tombstones.

She didn't fear the mountain anymore. She had learned not to fear many things, especially not to fear being alone. Why then this overwhelming sense of loneliness tonight? Lately, she was beginning to give in to weaknesses. This afternoon, for instance. This afternoon, Lucy had almost convinced her that Vic had really deserved the award . . . .

Below, Bella was barking disgracefully, her worshipful eyes raised to where Laura was standing. Poor baby! Laura knew she had been neglecting the little creature lately, and she felt very guilty. Taking the steep steps two at a time, she quickly worked her way down to the mansion's front stairs and caught Bella up in her arms, hugging and nuzzling the ecstatic dog. Squirming and yapping joyfully, Bella bounced from Laura's arms, begging to be chased. The moonlight was bright, and Laura decided to play a few games with the dog. Scooping up a twig from the ground, she turned and threw the improvised toy against the house. Sure enough, Bella took off in hot pursuit. Laura laughed at the happy creature's flight. That's when she first saw the murky figure standing and watching from the expanse of the veranda. Her imagination ran as wild as her pulse for a moment, but the dusky shadow could only be one person, of course.

Laura waited for Bella to drop the rescued twig at her feet before saying, "Good evening, Donna Evangelina." She threw the twig aloft again, and Bella bounded away. "Forgive me, but I didn't know you were here."

Laura's mother-in-law moved away from the corner of the veranda and walked slowly toward the steps. As usual, she was dressed in black from head to toe. Her expression remained as somber as her clothes. "Would you have avoided coming downstairs if you knew I was here?"

Laura let this pass without comment. "Tina told me you were ill. Are you feeling better?"

"Not really. My head will throb until this heat stops."

Bella came back, bearing the twig in her mouth. Sensing her mistress had lost interest in their game, she sadly waddled up the steps and plopped down on the veranda, her head nestled in her front paws. Laura approached the little creature and rubbed the dog's furry ears. "Perhaps," she said over her shoulder, "you might be more comfortable if you wore a lighter dress . . . ."

"I will honor my son's memory by wearing mourning until the day I die," she hissed, noting with open disgust that Laura wore nothing under her thin silk shirt. "Unlike his wife!"

Laura knew it would be useless to attempt to carry on a civil conversation, and she started for the front door. But Donna Evangelina grasped Laura's arm and held on to it with a hard, wild strength. "You would like nothing better than to get rid of me, wouldn't you? You would love to see me go back to Italy!"

"Signora, you know I will never force you to leave this house."

"Ah, yes, of course! You will never force me to leave because you promised Frank that if anything ever happened to him you would always take care of me, isn't that so?"

"Yes, and you know I will keep my promise."

"How thoughtful! How loving!" The harshness of her features was magnified as she brought her face closer to Laura's. "If only you had been a thoughtful and loving wife, perhaps my son would still be alive today!"

"You know his death was an accident. You know I had nothing to do with it!" Laura struggled in vain against that iron grip.

"Liar!" Her voice dropped to an oily whisper. Donna Evangelina couldn't contain her hatred any longer. "You ordered him to go out that night, and you were ecstatic when Beppo found his corpse!"

"That's insane! Signora, let go of me!" Until now, a cold animosity had always existed between the two women, but it was polite and guarded. Laura was amazed at this sudden outburst of naked hatred.

"Tell me, Lauretta," the old woman insisted, her grip like steel, "do you ever think of Frank? Do you remember him when you disappear for days in San Francisco—free, capricious, *alive*! Do you ever bother to think of your dead husband when you're whoring around like the bitch you really are?"

Laura yanked herself away, knowing she was going to be sick. She had never known the bile of real disgust before; now she felt herself choking on it. Sick and confused, she stumbled halfway down the steps and stopped, not really knowing what she was doing or where she was going. Every instinct told her to run, to get away from this house, or she wouldn't survive. But she couldn't see where to go. She was blinded by a light so strong it brought a cry from her lips. She flung her hands upward to protect her eyes as the light grew brighter and brighter. Then she heard the roar of the motor. After that, there was silence, and the darkness mercifully returned. "Vic?"

"Are you all right, Laura?"

Her eyes slowly adjusted to the darkness. He was wearing a white shirt that looked stark against the the shadows of his hands and face. "I'm all right." She took a deep breath and concentrated on every syllable. "You surprised me, that's all." None of this could be real! As Laura watched Vic slowly take a few steps closer, she heard the dry rasp behind her. It was all too real. "I don't think you know each other. Vic Remo, this is my mother-in-law, Signora Evangelina Spandoni."

Vic murmured a few polite words in Italian. Laura

marveled at how calmly Donna Evangelina answered, as polite and formal as if nothing had happened. Her mother-in-law inquired solicitously, "You're not from this area, are you, Mr. Remo? I don't remember seeing you before."

"No, Signora, I'm not."

"Ah, I see." The woman looked with frank malice from Vic to Laura. "Then you must be one of Lauretta's San Francisco . . . acquaintances."

Vic couldn't fathom the blank expression on Laura's face and decided to add nothing to the old woman's strange implication. But it seemed she wasn't waiting for an answer. "I see!" She began to walk rapidly to the front door, looking straight ahead. "My head is throbbing. I must go to my room."

With Donna Evangelina gone, Vic waited for Laura to break the awkward silence that followed. Her first words, however, were directed at Bella. "Stop that! Go into the house." The dog had been emitting a ghastly rumbling ever since Donna Evangelina had grabbed Laura, and the animal's nerves had not improved much since she had spied Vic.

With a sad glance at her mistress, Bella padded into the mansion. The idea of entering the house too and slamming the heavy oak door in Vic Remo's face occurred to Laura, but rather than take a coward's way out she summoned all her courage to rid herself of his disturbing presence once and for all. "You shouldn't have come out here to the Winery, Vic. I don't know why you won't leave me alone!"

That was not altogether true. Since they had first met, some sense had warned her to suspect his every move, his every gesture. She knew the Winery was at the heart of the matter. She had underestimated his intelligence and his tenacity. He had figured out that the aging wine would be reaching a critical stage at any moment now, and he had dashed out here expecting to find her desperate and quivering to sign over her land to Canova. Well, maybe some other woman might throw herself, helpless and sniveling, on his broad shoulders looking for an easy way out, but not Laura D'Asti!

"Why won't you understand that I can't sell my land? Stop haunting me! Leave me alone, and get out of my life!"

"Are you through giving orders?"

His tone left her speechless. Damn him! There was that arrogant, unrelenting forcefulness again! He shifted his body slightly. She found herself taking a step backward. Amazed, she could answer him only in a whisper. "Yes, that's all I have to say...."

"Now, keep still and listen to me. You know we have something to settle between us, Laura, and it has nothing to do with the Winery."

Oh, yes! She knew what he was talking about. Steeling herself, she leaned against the wooden balustrade next to the stairs. Her hand encountered cold dampness; ground fog was beginning to enshroud the Valley of the Moon.

"I don't know if I love you, but I intend to find out tonight." He walked calmly back to the car and opened the door. "Get in."

It wasn't too late; she could still go into the house and be safe. That is, she would be safe for tonight. But what about all the tomorrows? Without touching the chilled balustrade again, she came slowly down the steps. The rising miasma, as soft and white as cotton, clung to her legs. Glancing at Vic for a moment, she climbed into the car. It was after he had shut and locked the door securely behind her that she remembered she had sworn never to speak to him again.

CHAPTER SIX

The words remained in her mind: "I don't know if I love you, but I intend to find out . . . " Laura's mouth felt dry and her lips tightened remembering how Vic had looked when he murmured those words.

The knot in her stomach constricted as he shot the screaming car down the deserted Sonoma streets and then headed toward the sea. He had smashed her resolve so easily. This ridiculous escapade had to stop, but then she made the mistake of glancing at him at the exact moment he turned to her. All that was virile, strong, and handsome in his face was highlighted by the car's dim inner lights. She knew any resistance on her part would be a sham. His eyes demanded she remember that night in his apartment. That very first touch, that lingering, scorching caress had seeped through her aching body like hot quicksilver. How would it end tonight? With Vic, how could she be sure of anything? Oh, he would make love to her tonight. It was useless to pretend she didn't want him desperately But then, would she be left with her pride in shambles and her life shattered? No, not if she didn't fall in love with him . . .

He was still looking directly at her. "I never thought you'd be afraid of me."

"I'm not afraid of you." She swayed with the movement of the car. He turned back to look at the road and braked smoothly at the bottom of a steep curve. The beautiful machine leaped forward with each change of gears. They quickly reached the top of a ridge where Laura caught sight of the moon darting in and out of the tall redwoods lining the foggy, twisting road. "Is Carole afraid of you?"

"No," he murmured. It was a dead sound. The road had leveled, and he glanced at her again. "Forget about her. I'll admit Carole intrigued me for a while with some of her unusual talents, but that's all over." He was deliberately blunt so that he couldn't be misunderstood. "I never told her I loved her, Laura."

She wanted to believe him, but his words made her shudder. "Don't ever talk that way about me. Oh, please . . ."

"Never. I swear it. I would only be lying." He reached over to the backseat for his jacket and wrapped it around her trembling shoulders with his free hand. Suddenly the road began to climb again, and he reluctantly returned to shifting gears. But the uneven huskiness of his voice exposed the tension inside of him. "Come close to me. Hold me."

Bending sideways, she freed her arms from the warmth of his jacket and slowly curled her fingers through his hair before letting her hand fall to encircle his shoulders. Moving closer still, she let everything fly from her mind as she felt the sinews and cords of his neck and back flexing beneath her fingertips. The car continued to roll and swerve hypnotically. Neither of them spoke as the undulating countryside, caught in the flashing beams of the headlights, hurtled by. The trees were sparse now, and the moonlight had succumbed to fog and mist. "Where are you taking me?" she whispered.

"Where we can be completely alone. By the coast, near Inverness."

They were near the ocean now. Between the banks of fog she could see the silhouette of a village nestled on a spit of sand between the great, raging breakers of the Pacific and the calm waters of Tomales Bay. "Yes, I want to be with you alone . . . ."

Bracing himself to drive down the foggy incline that ended at the beach, he took hold of her wrist and placed her hand on his thigh. Each movement brought the muscles of his legs into a tight, bulging knot. Instinctively, her hand gripped him tighter. She began moving her palm across the fabric along his thigh. She continued the arousing, teasing gesture, knowing he had to keep both hands on the wheel.

"I could stop right here . . . ."

"No." She smiled. "Go on. Have we far to go?"

"I don't think so." He slowed the car down to a near crawl. "But I can't be sure in this thick fog."

About a mile farther on, he suddenly veered the car sharply to the left onto a dirt road that seemed to bisect a small forest. He nodded, satisfied he had found the right driveway. They were in a glen protected by dense foliage. In the distance, Laura could see a series of large, rustic cabins joined by a road that traveled up to what seemed to be a central lodge. Even in the clinging mist, the remote, isolated setting felt snug and secure.

Vic parked below the line of cabins. "Wait here for a second, okay?"

She nodded, and he was gone before she could hand him his jacket. She watched him climb up to the main lodge, his white shirt pale against the gray mist. Hugging the jacket closer around herself, she settled deeply into the seat and, shutting her eyes, leaned backward on the headrest. Completely alone. How many times, she wondered, had he been completely alone with somebody in this wild, romantic spot? Even in the thick fog, he had unerringly found the driveway. Hugging herself tighter still, she struggled to stop thinking like a fool. His private life was his own business, and he owed her no explanations. What did she expect, a full declaration of love and a proposal of marriage before he touched her?

"Let me help you. It's pretty dark out here." He was holding the door open. A large brass key dangled from his hand. She stepped out, and they walked slowly up a slippery graveled path, his arms clasped around her. They stopped in front of one of the cabins. Two glowing carriage lamps burned by the door of the cozy redwood building, and by their indirect light she glimpsed an improbable cluster of white roses nearby, all in full bloom. She instantly stretched her hand out to pluck one of the flowers.

"Careful," he warned. "The thorns are sharp. I'll pick one for you." He did so, and still holding the white bloom carefully near the top of the stem, he unlocked the cabin and let her pass inside.

Nothing on the outside of the cabin could have prepared her for the loveliness within. Vic leaned against the as she spun slowly around. "I expected rustic cha this is beautiful!" She smiled. Everything in high-beamed room was decorated in dark ton the inviting bed, which dominated a spacious corner. It was lavishly piled high with a white down comforter and many matching toss pillows. The only light in the room radiated from the big fireplace. It shone brightly enough for Laura. "Ah, I forgot all about my rose," she said, looking at Vic across the room.

As he slowly crossed the space between them, he began to strip the thorns from the stem of the flower, one by one, with his long, strong fingers. "Now it's perfect," he murmured, "almost as perfect as you are." He lifted the rose and laid it softly against her mouth. Then he drew it gently downward along the delicate curve of her neck until it came near the edge of her blouse. He snapped off the tiny buttons that held the thin material together and let the flower fall into the velvety niche between her breasts. With an impatience that made her cry out, he suddenly crushed the flower and flung the petals away, pressing his mouth to the same spot.

Laura had never felt anything so exquisite. Racked by what he was doing to her, she cast aside the last shred of restraint. Bending dizzily over him, she pulled his head back. Her lips were open and inviting. Her mouth ached to receive the same sweet hurt he was inflicting on the rest of her body. Instead, he stepped away. Swiftly, with a strange tenderness, he drew her over to the bed. Easing himself down on his back, he pulled her, unresisting, on top of him. Their bodies melded together perfectly. She could feel his heart pounding as he strained upward to kiss her eyelids and run his tongue along the lobe of her ear. He seemed to be feeding his hunger by lingering over every part of her body, but he was intent on avoiding her mouth. "You said I was to be selfish," she whispered, barely able to breath, "so I insist you kiss me!"

"That was the other night. Tonight I can't wait . . ."

She smiled at the naked need in his beautiful, sensuous eyes. "I don't care! I insist . . ." She broke off, bending way down and vexingly biting the corner of his mouth ever so lightly. She had bargained for a kiss, but she got much more than that. Fiercely, he pinned her to him with one arm, and with his free hand clutched her open blouse at the back of the neck and wrenched it down, trapping her arms behind her within its folds. Twisting so that she was now pressed hard beneath him, he finally took her mouth and kissed it violently. It was a kiss unlike any other they had ever savored together. And he kept demanding her mouth, again and again. Their response to each other was anything but automatic—it was urgent, it was convulsive, and it was completely consuming. Somewhere between excruciating pleasure and exquisite pain she thought she heard him moan, "I love you, Laura. I love you . . ." Perhaps she only imagined it, she yearned so much to hear him say exactly those words.

"Vic?" She awoke, confused and cold. She reached out, but he wasn't lying next to her. Then a light blazed, small at first, but finally full of warmth. She saw him kneeling by the fireplace, dusting off his hands. "That's better." He smiled, rushing back to bed.

"Ah, your skin's so cold!" she whispered, folding the downy comforter snugly around him. "Let me warm you." He placed her head on his shoulder and tightly held her there while she rubbed away the chill from his body. She felt him brush his palm across her brow as if to prove to himself that she was no illusion. She had to know. "You whispered 'I love you.' Did you mean it?"

"Yes." His palm circled her face, stroking the smooth skin with a tiny anxiety that gave lie to his even tone. "And you?"

She nodded, although it was too dark for him to see. "It's the first time I've said *I love you, darling* to anybody." Excited by the way his breathing changed, she continued to stroke the hard grooves of his chest and then his stomach. The rough hair clung to her fingers. "Is it morning yet?" The heavily draped windows shaded whatever light could have come into the room.

"No," he lied. "Don't stop . . . please . . ."

The first thing Laura saw as she stepped outside the cabin was a sky dotted with light, billowing clouds. All traces of the evening's mist had gone. The sun shone brilliantly, although the wind was sharp and brisk. She was very happy to have Vic's jacket, since her shirt had lost most of its buttons. Glancing sideways along the narrow patio that edged the cabin, she saw him turn the corner and walk toward her. She studied him carefully, remembering how he had looked in the semidarkness last night. He looked at her now with the same expression of love, and she was happy.

"I'm sorry : . ." were his first words, noticing her torn blouse.

"Don't be." She hesitated only for a moment and then rushed into his arms. "Beautiful, isn't it?" she said, enthralled with the fresh air and sunshine.

"Yes, you are." He kissed her very gently this time. "Come on, I want to show you something."

She followed him around to the other side of the patio and was instantly thrilled by the panorama. With his arms locked around her, they watched the breaking waves of the ocean become luminous and still as they entered the sheltered bay. What she had thought was a forest turned out to be a magnificent grove of redwoods, here since the dawn of history. The garden of the main lodge was a rainbow of colors, and birds sang from every tree. "I love to come here by myself to unwind," Vic said, capturing the strands of her burnished hair in his hand to keep them from flying wild in the wind, "but we'll come back here together from now on."

"Will we?" As delighted as she was to learn that he had shared all this untainted beauty with no one else, she had to fight a surging doubt about something else. How could she joyously think of the future when the problems at the Winery were so complex and insoluble? To make things worse, while others were feverishly working to solve the immediate problem of the vintage wine, she was miles away from the vineyard, indulging herself in Vic's love.

He felt the shudder that passed through her body. "You can't keep living with this weight on your shoulders. There's only one answer, Laura, and you know what it is. You must sell the Winery. No, wait." He drew his arms more tightly around her so she couldn't run away. "Listen to me! The vintage will have to be processed very soon now. You know that, don't you? What equipment will you use? How are you going to manage without money?"

"It's worse than that, Vic. Matt thinks it will peak in three days—at the most."

The low curse that rumbled from his throat surprised Laura. She couldn't doubt his sincerity any longer. Tilting her head so she could look directly at him, she said, "I want you to tell me the truth. If I signed the contract immediately selling Canova the Winery—" Her voice shook a little, but she willed herself to go on. "—would you promise me you could save the wine? Please, don't lie to me!"

He brushed her lips slowly with his. It was a reflex action, his brain was rapidly calculating, furiously sorting out complex procedures. "If I draw up the contract today, and Canova and you sign the papers tomorrow, I can have the necessary equipment installed in three days."

"But we may have less than three days!"

"Don't worry, I can hold the high essence of the wine in remission for a while once I take over the operation. It's very expensive and it's delicate work, but it can be done." He suddenly swung her around and cupped her face in his hands. "Laura, darling," he pleaded, "you'd be doing what's best for us, too! We can't have this conflict standing between us."

She clutched his hands, praying she was making the right decision, fighting back the burning tears. She could feel the spot on his palm where Bella's fangs had pierced through the flesh. The wound was still noticeable but healing. Below that, where Carole had once affixed a different brand, his wrist was bare. She hadn't noticed until this moment! "Yes, I'll sell."

Neither could speak. They remained clinging to each other. A few minutes later, they left the cabin and quickly reached the car. "I love you," he whispered, bending forward to switch on the ignition. "I also love it when you're sitting very close to me, remember?"

Putting one arm around his shoulder and the other tightly around his waist, she leaned on him and sighed. "I won't have to give up the house, will I?"

"No. I'll insist on that and a few other important points. Let me worry about it, Laura." The motor roared to full thrust, and he guided the car carefully over the narrow dirt road. Once they reached the highway, he gunned the car free and headed east, cutting through the barren Marin hills and leaving the redwoods far behind. Only a bent cypress came into view now and then. Soon they were in the Petaluma dairy country where grazing herds peacefully congregated in sheltering coves. Vic peered down. Laura's head was still nestled warmly on his shoulder. "Asleep?"

"No, just thinking. I must tell Tina and Matt about selling the Winery. And Beppo . . . and my mother-in-law."

His jaw clenched tautly. Ah, yes, Donna Evangelina. He meant to rid Laura of that problem, too, but he had to tread carefully. "I've been thinking, too. When all this is over and you've had the time to rest and to think clearly, why don't you consider reopening the tasting room to the public again? It's a shame to keep it closed. That room is very important in the history of Napa-Sonoma." He kept his eyes pinned on the road ahead. "Why did you close the room? It could have brought money into the Winery." He forged on. "Laura, how did your husband die?" He heard her gasp and clasped one of her hands, squeezing it so hard he thought he felt her small bones cracking. "I'm so sorry," he moaned. "I have no right to ask you such a thing."

"No, darling, you have every right."

Gently lifting her bruised hand to his lips, he kissed it. "In that case, you'd better tell me."

"Yes," she murmured, "and then maybe I can forget the whole tragic story. It happened so fast, really. The rain had been drenching the ground for days and days. It never stopped! We were all worried, not only about the vines being ruined by the constant moisture, but also about the extraordinary wine beginning to mellow in the casks."

Surprised, Vic glanced down at Laura's haunted face. "I don't understand. How were the casks in danger?"

"The cellars are well belowground, remember? The buildings are old and in poor condition. It wasn't uncommon for the rain to flood the floors. We had pumps, but they were old and useless. My father planned to buy new ones. Then he died, and there was no money." She took a deep breath, grateful that he reached over to clutch her even more tightly. The road had straightened for a stretch. "But we couldn't control the flooding from this rain. We were having supper, and I was frantic about the water infiltrating the casks or rotting the wood and having them burst open. Frank was even more worried, and he left to check the cellars. After he had a terrible argument with his mother, that is! She insisted the wine wasn't worth his going out into such a storm! She couldn't understand how valuable that wine would become, and she always dominated him. But he went. He never came back."

Vic had taken a shortcut from Petaluma that lead directly to the D'Asti acreage in Sonoma. He brought the car to a fast stop at the gate and swiftly gathered Laura in his arms. "Go on. What happened?"

"After an hour, when he still hadn't returned, I ran to the cellars myself. As I went through the tasting room to reach the cellars, I saw Beppo kneeling. He was holding Frank's body in his arms. Beppo had been worried about the casks, too. He had passed through the tasting room and found my husband already dead." She pushed herself away from him and turned to look at the lush land beyond. Her land until tomorrow. "I'll never know how the accident happened. I can only guess that Frank Spandoni slipped on the uneven stone floor, fell, and . . ." Unable to stifle the sobs any longer, she cried, "Vic, he drowned in only a few inches of water!"

He didn't try to stop her sobbing; the tears were long overdue. The best thing he could do was to let the sobs and the pent-up, incoherent words spill out until all the frustration, doubt, and guilt had been wrung from her heart. Finally, gasping one last time, she tried to wipe the tears from her cheeks with a futile, childlike gesture. He reached into the pocket of his jacket, which she still wore, and took out a handerchief. "Thanks," she said, striving to smile. "I'm afraid it'll take more than this to undo the damage I've done to my face."

She spent the next few seconds dabbing at her eyes. When she was calm again, he slowly turned her face away from the window. He bent over so that their foreheads gently touched. "First of all," he murmured, "your face looks beautiful, and secondly, I don't ever want you to suffer and cry like this again. That's an order, understand?"

"Yes, sir!" she jested, closing her eyes, which were still full of pain. "But . . ."

"No, Laura, I'm serious. The nightmare is over. Or it will be over when you deal with Donna Evangelina. Look, she's been taking advantage of you. I saw the tension between the two of you last night, and I can easily guess how she's been torturing you about her son's death. Give her the respect she deserves, but stop letting her rule your life. Frank Spandoni's death was an accident, pure and simple. You don't owe Donna Evangelina a damned thing!"

Laura listened quietly. She knew he was right. She had allowed the woman complete freedom with everything that belonged to Tina and herself—money, the house, even the vineyards—and the malicious creature had enjoyed everything without a word of gratitude or kindness. On the contrary, her mother-in-law seemed capable of spewing out only hate and dirt. Well, Donna Evangelina would have to learn to adjust to a different life, just as she herself would have to learn to live differently. "I have to find Tina and Matt, Vic. Then I promise I'll speak to my mother-in-law." She shook her head when he reached to start the car. "No, I think I'll walk to the house from here. I want a little time to myself before . . . before I tell everyone about selling the Winery. Do you understand?"

"I understand, but I want to go with you."

"No. I have to take care of this my own way. But thank you, darling," she said, kissing him quickly and slipping out of the car. "Will you call me tonight?"

"Of course. I'll dash back to my apartment, change, and then tackle Canova and hammer out a contract. I'll phone you as soon as I return home." He demanded another kiss. Then he turned the car around, waved, and headed toward San Francisco.

Laura paused, leaning on the wooden gate that guarded the entrance to the road. She gazed abstractly across the fields, blocking any pangs of self-pity from changing her mind. She knew down to the very depths of her soul that she had made the right decision. She let her hand slip to her side and found a familiar wet nose nudging it. Bella had come out to greet her. Faithful Bella! Laura leaned down to pat the dog on the head. They spoke in a fond language intelligible only to the two of them. The joyous dog followed as Laura walked slowly down the dirt lane, her head bowed and her eyes on the ground. She didn't want to dwell on memories of last night. Later, after she had broken the news of the Winery's sale to everybody, she would lock herself in her room and relive every tenderness and touch, every exciting and fulfilling moment she had shared with Vic. But not now. A playful bark from Bella caused her to look up. She had nearly reached the house; the arbor loomed nearby. Parked directly ahead was a big, luxurious, custom-made car. It took a few dizzy seconds before she noticed the personalized license plate read Carole.

CHAPTER SEVEN

Carole Canova. *Here?* Why? Vic, of course. Carole's feminine intuition must have been working overtime since the night he had unceremoniously left her stranded at the opera. What could Carole expect to gain by coming to the Winery? Did she hope for a vulgar screaming match with Vic as the prize? Annoyed rather than angry, Laura ran up the front steps feeling strong enough to face anybody this morning. Vic loved her and she loved him. It was so simple, really. Almost at the top step, she swung around and gazed at the lovely morning. There had been both moonlight and fog on the lawn last night when Vic had stood there. But a few hours had changed everything—and Frank Spandoni's ghost had been banished forever!

Inside, the house was cool and quiet. Tina was probably in the cellars working with Matt. Laura resisted the temptation to run over there immediately. First, Carole Canova! Where was Donna Evangelina this morning? she wondered. Still pampering her convenient headache? Just as well; Laura hoped her mother-in-law would stay locked in her room until later. Donna Evangelina had probably been spying from the upstairs window last night, and nothing but accusations and sarcasm could be expected from her now.

Laura grimly crossed the spacious hallway on her way to the formal front parlor where she suspected Carole was waiting, arrogant and cold. Before she reached the parlor door, she heard the merriest of laughs from the direction of the breakfast room. She stopped dead in her tracks. Although she had never heard her laugh in such a frivolous way before, Laura was positive it was Donna Evangelina! Urging herself not to hurry, she walked to the breakfast room and there remained standing in the doorway, astounded by the sight in front of her eyes. The wrought-iron breakfast table had been elegantly set with flowers, and seated across from each other, smiling and laughing, were Donna Evangelina and Carole Canova. They seemed to be getting on famously, taking turns dipping delicate fingers into a mound of freshly baked *biscotti* and sipping daintily from cups brimming with hot frothy *cioccolata*. Laura's astonishment quickly turned to anger when she recognized the breakfast table's other embellishments. Everything from the old ivory lace tablecloth and napkins to the beautiful, wafer-thin Florentine chocolate set had belonged to her mother and had been left as a loving gift to Tina and herself. Cherished and priceless, the antique D'Asti linen and china had been traditionally used only for the happiest family occasions—a betrothal, a wedding, a birth, a baptism. Neither sister would have dreamed of using the treasured articles for anything other than the most momentous occasions. Yet Donna Evangelina had disdainfully decided to use the china and linen to entertain Carole Canova! The green-and-white room was warm with sunshine, yet Laura felt a chill that struck right down to her bones. She rubbed the numbing coldness away from her arms still covered with Vic's jacket.

"Ah, Lauretta, my dearest child," Donna Evangelina said. Her eyes sparkling with malice, she dabbed gently at her mouth with a napkin. "I see you've finally found your way home!" She nodded in a convivial way toward Carole, then returned to Laura. "In your regrettable absence, I've been entertaining Mr. Remo's charming fiancée. We've been having such a delightful morning. Miss Canova has told me some very interesting stories about Vic Remo, and I've been telling her some interesting things about you, dear."

Laura wasn't the least bit concerned about the lies her mother-in-law had probably been spreading, but she did wonder which of the two woman had decided on the term *fiancée*. No doubt, it had been Donna Evangelina. Morality was more her style. But her mother-in-law couldn't hurt her anymore, not after Vic had opened her eyes to the pathetic woman's tricks. Laura curbed her temper and turned to the cool Carole instead. "If you had phoned earlier, you could have saved yourself the trip." There was no attempt to be polite.

"Oh, but I did call," Carole murmured, as innocent as the morning's light. "When Donna Evangelina couldn't find you in your bedroom," she continued, with a slight emphasis on the word *your*, "she graciously invited me to come out to the Winery anyway. She was sure you would show up eventually."

Enjoying every moment of her daughter-in-law's supposed discomfort, Donna Evangelina rose like a reigning queen and poured Carole some more chocolate. "Yes,

Lauretta, I knew you would surely return sometime today because of all that fuss over the wine you've so foolishly allowed to spoil." Her sweet smile turned back to Carole. "I always say a woman has no right to meddle in men's work. A woman's only satisfaction should come from being a loving wife and mother, don't you agree, Miss Canova?"

"Absolutely," Carole purred with complete conviction.

Donna Evangelina's smiled remained, but it turned brittle and ugly. "I was really too ill to notice, Lauretta, but wasn't that Mr. Remo who left the house with you last night?"

Laura wasn't about to blurt out some stupid answer. Instead, she strolled to the table and very deliberately sat down on the chair just vacated by her mother-in-law. "Yes, and Vic drove me back this morning." She was slightly puzzled by the way Carole's eyes narrowed warily, but her thoughts didn't linger for long. She swiftly zeroed in on her mother-in-law. "I think I will have some chocolate, too." She didn't lift a finger to help herself, and after an awkward pause, Donna Evangelina was forced to pour a fresh cup of chocolate. The old woman was irate, and Laura knew it. She let her stew and stirred up the froth in the cup that had been slammed in front of her. "It's true, you have been so ill. I'd feel very guilty if I kept you from your bed any longer. Thank you for entertaining Miss Canova, but now I really must insist you think of your health." She took her time drinking some of the hot liquid. "Good morning, Signora."

The dismissal was so final that the tyrannical old woman was speechless. She wavered, her dark form a discordant shadow in the sunshine of the room. Her hands pressed down on the ivory tablecloth. Finally, she managed to pull herself together sufficiently to nod stiffly to Carole; she frigidly ignored Laura. Her black dress rustling, her back stiff as a rod, Donna Evangelina stalked out of the room.

Now Laura could concentrate on Carole. The proud heiress didn't look too well, although her hair, make-up, and clothes all testified to the fact that she had spent a huge amount of time grooming herself. At what ungodly hour had she begun to fuss with herself? Laura wondered, glancing across at the expensive raw-silk lounge suit. Carole's shoes and purse exactly matched the beige of her clothes and were crafted from the softest Milanese leather. In place of diamonds, Carole's throat was encased in creamy pearls, no less beautiful. Yet no amount of skillfully applied cosmetics could hide the murky circles under the violet eyes, nor could the smooth shine of the vibrant blond hair distract from the certainty that those same sensual eyes had not slept much last night. But Carole Canova remained the total picture of poise nevertheless, her lithe body leaning comfortably back in the chair, the small pout of disdain perched permanently on her lips. She gazed back at Laura in a sophisticated, practiced manner. Her own hair was disheveled, her blouse torn, her face devoid of make-up, Laura allowed Carole all the time necessary to look her over and fill in the missing pieces. Then she slowly took off Vic's jacket and asked, "How did you know Vic had been out here last night?"

Carole wasn't disturbed by the question. "I waited for him in his apartment as usual. When he didn't show up, I began to think. He's been a little less than attentive lately, and I know his patterns very well. I remembered the pictures of Vic splashed all over the papers yesterday after he won some kind of award from the wine industry.

In most of the photos he appeared very interested in a certain brunette who must have given him that stupid award with her own little hands. Then I remembered where I had seen that particular brunette before! I saw you the opening night of the opera, of course, the same night Vic left me high and dry! I never listen when Vic and my father talk business—it bores me—but I've heard them discuss the name D'Asti quite a bit lately, so-o-o . . ." She smiled, rather pleased with her own cleverness. "While I waited for Vic in vain last night, I called my father, wormed out of him the info that the D'Astis live in Sonoma, and the rest was easy. It wasn't hard to figure out that Vic was trying to coax you into a hot little affair, Laura. As I said, I know his habits, and I know how persuasive he can be, professionally and personally—"

"So you called this morning, talked to my foolish mother-in-law—"

"That foolish woman was a gold mine of information."

"And then you dashed out here determined to pull a hysterical scene. Sorry to disappoint you, but Vic dropped me off at the main gate. Don't jump to the wrong conclusions—I'm not trying to hide him from anybody—I just wanted to be by myself for a while." She shied away from confessing to the sale of the Winery, however. The part of Carole's story about Vic's persuasiveness, professionally *and* personally, had hit too close for comfort. "You've wasted nothing but time coming out here to see me."

"I don't think so," Carole said, suprisingly. "Maybe it's just as well that I didn't run into Vic, after all. I don't see why we can't settle this little mess between us in a very civilized manner."

"What are you talking about?" Laura impatiently got up and went over to the window that faced the Winery's processing buildings. The structures housing the cellars were just visible in the distance. She remembered that Tina and Matt were still hard at work down there. "What do you really want?"

"All right, Laura D'Asti," Carole said in a very different tone. "I'll stop being subtle and spell it out for you. I don't think you're anybody's fool, especially after seeing how you pulled the claws out of your hideous mother-in-law! But let's talk about Vic. He can't help it, he was born with a chemistry that can get under a woman's skin and itch her to death. Don't look so prissy and shocked; you know damned well what I'm talking about! And, Laura, darling, so do a lot of other women! I've been able to keep his interest so far, but I know he was also born with a built-in defense system. Haven't you found out yet that he's highly allergic to marriage?" For the first time, she let down her guard for a second. "I've stomped on my pride and looked the other way a few times. With other women, I mean. But you're different. I think you could be a very serious problem." She reached for her purse and took out a small, flat calfskin checkbook. Signing her name and leaving the rest blank, she tore the check from its binder and placed it on the side of the table closest to Laura. "I don't know if you're being forced to sell this depressing little farm or not—I couldn't care less, believe me—but I know that no woman can ever have enough money! Be sensible, darling. I know what Vic's worth, so don't be shy about filling out a nice big figure. Of course, in return, I expect you to live up to your end of our little bargain. You know what that is, don't you? I simply never want you to see him again!"

Laura didn't touch the piece of paper. She stared at the loathsome thing as if she expected it to jump off the table and bite her. "Why?" The word almost choked her. "**Why are you groveling like this for somebody who doesn't love you? Oh, no,**" she protested, cutting Carole off. "**I know he doesn't love you! You don't love him, either.**" She snatched the blank check from the table, crushed it in her fist until it was a tight ball, and then threw it with all her strength at Carole's face. "Or you wouldn't degrade him this way!"

The crushed paper glanced off Carole's cheek and fell harmlessly to her lap. She just left it there. "Love? I didn't say anything about love."

"Then why are you fighting so hard to keep him?"

Carole picked up the check and held it aloft, shaking her head in disbelief. "Sure you won't change your mind? Oh, don't be so damned moral. You're not the first of Vic's toys I've paid off, and you won't be the last. You need the money, and to be perfectly honest with you, he'll tire of you soon enough. You're simply not in his league." Laura's disgust must have been apparent. Carole finally shrugged and dropped the crushed check back into her purse. "I'll tell you why I want him all to myself," she whispered hoarsely. "There are other things more important to me than love and romance. Sex, for instance. Oh, I manage to keep him amused, too. . . ."

Laura recalled the only other time she had seen Carole. Lucy had said "Underneath all that glamour Carole Canova's just your nice, average, normal nympho." And only a few hours ago, Vic himself had admitted "Carole intrigued me for a while with some of her unusual talents." How sad! Laura looked at Carole—so refined, so glamorous—and wondered why she only felt sadness. All the anger had drained away, and she was grateful that she felt no smugness or sense of superiority. How could she and not be a complete hypocrite? Yet there had been a tenderness, a feeling of love last night between Vic and herself that somehow made it different.

"Don't tell me you're letting yourself fall in love with him?" Carole accused, sensing what was going through Laura's mind. "Then I was wrong. You're not a fool— you're crazy!" She jumped from the chair and came close to Laura. "I know he's charming and irresistible, but don't let his skill as a lover turn your stupid little head. What did he do"—she laughed, but it was an unpleasant sound —"let you have the full, hot Sicilian treatment with the cozy café, candles, and homemade wine? Or was it more exotic and wild—a stormy coast hideaway with howling winds—?"

"*Shut up!*" Laura yearned to slap that mouth. "For your own sake, shut up! I'm sick of your lies about him, and I'm sick of you! You found your own way into my house, now find your own way out. Right now!"

"Laura?"

How long had her sister been standing there? Laura wondered, spinning around. Matt was with Tina, and they had a stranger with them. Of the trio, the strange man seemed to be the most startled. But he wasn't looking at Laura; Carole claimed all his attention. Thrown off-balance, Laura said the first thing that came into her mind. "I was just about to go and find you, Tina. You, too, Matt." She rounded the table, ignoring Carole, who had swiftly turned away from everyone to stare out the window. "Let's go outside," Laura urged. "I have something serious to tell both of you." But what about this stranger? She certainly couldn't tell Tina and Matt she had decided to sell the Winery in front of an audience, could she? Who was he?

Tina kept staring openly, first at Laura and then at Carole. Before she could ask anything, Matt silenced her by lightly touching her hand. "Just a moment, Tina. Let me explain everything to Laura, okay?" Surprisingly, Tina submitted without a protest.

Carole remained by the window, her body as stiff as a slab of marble. The unknown man seemed just as immovable. Laura was forced to suggest diplomatically, "Can't we wait to talk?"

"Sorry, we can't." Matt's earnest face wouldn't permit any opposition or interruption. "Tina and I have been knocking our brains out since dawn trying to figure out a way to keep that wine in remission, but all we've come up with is a big, blank zero."

There was no implied rebuke in his remark, but Laura felt awful about having left them to wrestle with the problem alone. At dawn she had not given the Winery a thought, wrapped in a mantle of warmth from the fire Vic had built just before he had come back to bed to gather her up in his arms again. "I'm sorry, I should have been there to tell you . . ." She hesitated. She had almost made a terrible blunder. How could she possibly tell them about the sale of the Winery at Vic's recommendation with Carole in the room? "What I meant to say is, I should have been there to help you."

"It wouldn't have mattered, Laura. You couldn't have changed the results."

His urgency was infectious. "Tell me," she insisted. She forgot all about her appearance, which had certainly not passed Tina's notice, nor Matt's, either, and became totally involved in what he was trying to tell her. "What's happened to the wine?"

"We have to bottle it immediately or we'll lose it. There's no other way, believe me."

"But that's not true." She had almost uttered Vic's name. "I was told it could be held in this critical stage for a number of days."

"Only with special equipment. The wine's essence has peaked, Laura. If we neglect it now, you'll never again be able to produce something as fine as The Eye of the Falcon. Sure, you'll have a first-rate wine, but it won't be *supreme*. Don't you understand?"

Shaken, she realized she had waited too long before taking Vic's advice. He had said it would take three days to bring in the necessary equipment to save the wine at its peak. Three days! She didn't have three days. "Are you positive, Matt?"

He turned and nodded toward the other man. "If you don't believe me, ask Bill Hoyt. He's the finest chemical field expert I know. Tina and I decided to ask his advice, and he's taken his own tests this morning. Tell her, Bill."

"It's true, Miss D'Asti." As Bill Hoyt reinforced Matt's theory in a straightforward, practical manner, Laura took the chance to study him a little more closely. He still kept Carole captured in the corner of his eye. Rugged yet not unattractive, he had the air of a man who knew what he was talking about and who could be trusted. "In my opinion, using the old methods, you should begin operations immediately. I'll give you all the help I can, Miss D'Asti. We may not be able to save the whole batch, but—"

"But at least we can save some of it!" Tina hadn't been able to keep quiet any longer. "Sis, what's the matter with you? Why are you hesitating? Aren't you even going to thank Bill for all the free help he'll be giving us?"

"Yes, of course. Thanks so much, Bill." She had made

up her mind. She knew she couldn't wait for Vic to take the problem off her shoulders, not if the wine was to be salvaged in supreme condition. There was nothing he could do now to help her, and it was entirely her own fault. She would still sell the Winery to Canova, but this vintage had to be saved! She would phone Vic later and explain everything. Surely, he would understand she had been left with no other choice. "Yes, let's go ahead with it!"

Tina let out a shout of glee and threw her arms around Matt's shoulders. He didn't seem to mind. "We have to contact farmers all over Sonoma. I'm sure we'll have no shortage of volunteers." The D'Asti family had helped many a distressed farmer in the Valley of the Moon over the years; support would be generous now that a D'Asti needed help. "We can begin this evening and work around the clock, if necessary."

"I'll call Lucy. Maybe she can lend a hand, too," Tina said, not lessening her hold on Matt one inch.

Laura had caught Tina's enthusiasm, and she smiled at her sister and Matt. He remained outwardly as serious as ever, but there was an unexpected gleam in his sandy eyes. How had Tina beguiled him so quickly? Laura wondered. She also was curious about something else. "I'm very appreciative, Bill, but I'd like to know why you're doing this for me."

The rugged man thought his answer over carefully. "When this vintage is issued, it'll make history in the world of wine. I'd like to remember that I played a small part in making it all happen. It's as simple as that, Miss D'Asti."

In the emotion-charged silence that followed this sincere statement, Carole Canova's gutteral voice slashed through the room like a blasphemy. "Oh, no, Bill Hoyt, it's not as simple as that!"

Absorbed by the exciting project ahead, Laura had forgotten about Carole. She watched, bewildered, as Carole snatched up her purse and ran wildly across the room, stopping abruptly only when she reached the doorway where Bill was standing. "You've waited a long time to get even with my father, haven't you? Revenge! Is that what you want, Bill? Or do you just want to hurt me?"

"I've never wanted to hurt you, Carole."

"Don't lie!" She gave him a last withering look and then fled.

Tina was flabbergasted; Matt seemed more than mildly shocked. Laura recovered first. "I've been told you're a fine chemist, and you've just explained to me that you respect what my family has accomplished," she said. "But what I really want to know is, who are you?"

"Laura," Matt interrupted again insistently, "your sister has told me all about Canova's rotten plan to buy you out. I'm glad you told him and Vic Remo, too, to go to hell. Regardless, I asked Bill to help us. I trust his knowledge, and I trust him."

The irony of his words about Canova and Vic made Laura cringe, but this wasn't the time to confess the truth. Afterward, when the wine had been saved, she would face the issue. Now she concentrated on Bill Hoyt. There was a mystery here, and she didn't like mysteries. "Shouldn't I trust you too, Bill?"

"I hope you can, especially after I tell you I'm probably laying both my career and my job on the line by offering my services to this project. I'm Ricardo Canova's chief chemist."

She looked from Matt to Tina to Bill again. All three

seemed to be holding their breaths. There was an honesty about the man she simply couldn't doubt. And Matt trusted him. But a piece of the puzzle was still missing. "The importance of the vintage isn't the only reason you're defying Canova, is it?"

"No," he readily admitted. "Canova has needed my expertise, and I've enjoyed being a top field-dog with his organization. I do have an old score to settle with him, that's true. But that's something that I'll deal with later. Take my word for it, Miss D'Asti, one thing has nothing to do with the other."

She believed him. "Matt's faith in you is enough for me. Let's get to work!"

Vic was exhausted, yet he felt an exhilaration about what he had accomplished for Laura today. He slipped the latchkey into the lock and walked slowly into his apartment. As he crossed the large room, turning on lights along the way, he undid his tie and eased open the collar button. Should he phone her immediately to tell her the good news, or should he have a well deserved drink first? Bending over the phone on his desk, he reached into his pocket and drew out Canova's contract. He had fought hard to win every concession for Laura: she'd keep the house, all present employees would be retained, and the Winery would always bear the D'Asti name. Another bonus was a trust fund for Tina's education. A smile fluttered across his tired, angular features. Yes, Laura would be pleased. Laura. He had been engrossed all day long in settling her finances and shaping her future, too busy to think about the real Laura—as she had been last night, glowing in the firelight, her copper hair flared on the pillow and spilling over his arm. He reached for the phone.

"Vic, darling? What are you doing? I've been waiting for you for hours!"

The bedroom door was slightly open, and he gave it a little push. A trail of discarded clothing—a silk skirt, a blouse, a leather pump, a wispy lace bra—dotted the surface of the thick carpet. What appeared to be a strand of creamy pearls lay right in the middle of the clutter. He picked it up and tossed it on the bed. "Your father must have cashed in a bundle for that little trinket. Don't you think you should stop being so careless with his expensive bribes?"

Carole stretched on the bed, playfully poking at the pearls with her toe. "If I lost it, Dad would just buy me another one. It's not a bribe, either. Dad just loves giving me gifts." She turned on her side, not bothering to pull the sheet up too high. "Where have you been all day?"

"At my office. Some of us work for a living, believe it or not."

"I called your private number all afternoon, and there was no answer."

"I was in the conference room with your father," he murmured, quickly tiring of the whole scene. "Take a break, Carole." He turned away and began to take off his clothes. "You're starting to sound like a wife."

Swallowing the ugly response his sarcasm deserved, she settled back in the large bed and watched him, enjoying his every movement and relishing the sight of his well-proportioned, potent body. The longer she watched, the deeper she sank into the bed. "I'm willing to forgive you, even though you've been treating me miserably, darling. . . ." She was whispering, but her voice was more serious than teasing.

"How long do you intend to keep playing this stupid game?"

"I don't think of it as a game. I'm very serious."

"So am I. I'm tired of all this cuteness, Carole. I've told you from the beginning we had nothing going for us, and now I'm telling you again. It's over."

"I don't like being dismissed like an ordinary slut, Vic!"

"Stop it." He wasn't angry; they had been over this too many times.

She sat up, frantic. "What would you like me to do now? Am I supposed to bow out gracefully, saying 'Thanks so much for everything, lover'?" Her voice rose shrilly. "What do you expect me to do?"

"You're missing the whole point, Carole. I really don't care what you do."

It was the cold way he said it that finally made her snap. "You bastard!"

If she had gambled for a reaction, she was brutally disappointed. The only sound she heard was a rapid spray as water beat against the marbled floor and walls of the shower. Clutching her knees, she waited bent forward on the bed, for him to come back into the bedroom. Her fury was mounting. Finally, the water stopped, but then the dull drone of an electric shaver reached her ears. After what seemed a horrible eternity, that noise ceased, too. She couldn't curb her anger, however, and made sure her words penetrated into the bathroom beyond. "I went to see Laura D'Asti today!"

"What?" He stood in the doorway, the towel clutched in his fist. "Why?"

His suppressed temper was about to break loose. For the first time, she was suddenly frightened. Her gaze slithered over to her purse, which still contained the crushed check. *No.* He must never know about that check! Lifting her chin with false defiance, she said, "Simple female curiosity, that's all. I know you've been seeing her, darling, so don't deny it."

"Why should I deny it?" His voice was pleasant and low, but his eyes were contemptuous. "What did you tell her, Carole?"

"Nothing!" She cursed herself for bringing up Laura. She had only wanted him to know she was aware of his deceit, but now he was very angry. She tried to think her way out of this dangerous trap, and then she remembered Bill Hoyt. He had been at the Winery today. Why? Some wine was spoiling. That was it. She began to laugh from sheer relief, knowing she had hit upon the perfect subterfuge. "But your precious Laura had some very interesting things to say," she spat out. "You're supposed to buy her rotting old farm for my father, aren't you?"

"Yes."

"Has she signed the contract yet?"

"No."

"But she has promised to sell?"

"Yes." The anger threatened to explode at any moment. She savored her triumph as long as she dared. "Darling, I'm afraid your earthy little widow is a cheat. While I was there, she gave orders to begin bottling some very special wine immediately. It was all very secretive and urgent. I'll bet she didn't tell you! I have a feeling neither you nor Dad are supposed to know anything about this. Vic, darling, I think you're about to be double-crossed!"

His response to this juicy tidbit was not at all what she had hoped. The anger left his face, and he instantly looked startled and then very worried. As if she didn't exist, he reached into the closet and hurriedly pulled on a tight pair of jeans. Next, he slipped a turtleneck sweater over his head and then deftly donned a pair of boots. He was halfway out the door before her sharp cry stopped him. "Where are you going?"

"You still haven't gotten the message, have you?" With no emotion whatsoever, he told her, "Look, as long as you're here, why waste the whole evening? There are some steaks in the refrigerator and a few bottles of champagne in the chiller. Make yourself at home. And, Carole, when you're finished, why don't you take back all that jewelry you gave me. It's expensive stuff, and I won't be wearing it anymore. You can leave the key to the apartment on my desk afterward. You won't be needing that anymore, either."

After the door had slammed shut, she fought back the urge to smash something against the wall. This was no time for hysteria; this called for cunning. So it was over. Now what? She knew she couldn't bear to be alone. Stepping out of bed and gathering her clothes, she seriously considered a number of possibilities. The answer, when it came, was so simple that she was a little stunned. Picking up the phone from the night table, she dialed the D'Asti number, praying that someone other than Laura would answer. Her luck held. An unknown voice said, "Hello." Thank God! She had probably reached one of the volunteers who had swarmed to the Winery to help save that stupid wine. Now that she couldn't back out, her voice shook slightly. "May I speak to Bill Hoyt, please."

He abandoned the sports car in the midst of a ridiculous variety of dilapidated vehicles and ran directly to the interlocking buildings at the far end of the vineyards. Passing swiftly through the door of the tasting room, Vic remembered the tragedy that happened in this room, an accident that had haunted Laura's life ever since. She'd never see ghosts here again, he vowed, standing firmly in the center of the chilly gloom.

"Darling, I'm not afraid of this room anymore," a voice whispered.

He spun around and saw her framed by the lights from the cellars below. "Laura!" She was so lovely.

She stood poised indecisively. Her surprise yielded to joy, and she rushed to be crushed in his arms. "I wanted so desperately to see you tonight!"

"I couldn't wait until tomorrow." With or without Carole's idiotic interference, he knew he would have been compelled to touch her and to hold her like this tonight.

"Carole was here this morning . . . ."

"I know. I found her waiting for me when I got home."

Laura looked up and waited for her pulse to stop its rapid beating. "Is it really over?"

"I told you last night." He worked his fingers through her hair and gripped hard. "She won't be bothering us again. We struck a bargain, about a half ton of gold jewelry in exchange for the key to my apartment."

Even though she didn't quite succeed in hiding the sigh that floated to her lips, she did say, "Let's never mention her again." Nor would she tell him about that awful business of the blank check. What would be gained?

But Vic said, "She did tell me you had ordered the vintage processed and bottled. Why?"

"I was going to phone you, but so many details have come down on my shoulders."

"Answer me, Laura. Why?"

Weary and distraught, she leaned harder against him. "Matt took new tests early this morning. The wine has peaked, and it will rapidly begin to decline. We've run out of time, Vic."

"Are you sure Matt's right?" He stepped away, although he still held onto her arms in a viselike grip. "If he's wrong, with the antiquated equipment you have down there, you're going to lose most of the wine. I don't care how many people will lend a hand, it just won't work." He let go of her. "In three days, with modern equipment, I could have saved the whole batch. Unless . . ." He remembered the contract he had left in the car and how hard he had fought with Canova to gain so much for Tina and her. But he wisely didn't talk about it and went on to ask her, "You've changed your mind about selling?"

"No, of course not," she said, casting a guilty glance over her shoulder toward the cellars, "but . . ."

He took a guess. "But you haven't told Tina or the others about the sale yet, right?"

"I didn't have time!" Why didn't he believe her? Didn't he know the agony she was experiencing? "Anyway, Matt's tests have been confirmed by Bill Hoyt."

"Hoyt? Canova's chemist? I don't get it." He had been caught off guard, and he didn't like it. "How did Hoyt get mixed up in this?"

"Matt asked for his advice because he has faith in his chemical know-how. Bill wants to help even if it costs him his job. Vic, you won't fire him, will you?"

"Do you think I might?"

"I don't know what to think!" She found herself walking farther from him and nearer to the steps of the cellars. "I believed only you would really understand why I had to save even a few bottles of that wine." Close to tears, she still refused to beg. "It's a joke on me, isn't it? Instead, everyone else but you seems to understand!"

"Laura!" His long strides caught up with her before she reached the steps. "Your happiness is the only thing that matters to me. If you don't believe me, I'd better leave right now and never come back. If you have any trust in me, you'll let me make a very simple, quick test of my own now. Then I'll give you my opinion of the condition of the vintage. If I honestly believe the bottling must begin immediately, I'll do it right now and I promise to save the whole lot."

"But how in God's name—?"

"I asked you to trust me. I must direct the entire operation, and I must be the only person giving orders."

Much more than the precious wine was at stake, she knew. Their future together depended on her answer. He wasn't testing her love; he already knew how intensely she loved him. He was waiting to find out if she would wipe away the remembrance of the many times she had caused him pain. That hideous moment in his apartment, for instance, when she had been so superior and stupid. And then her outrage when she had been convinced that he had not merited the Amici Award!

Her total trust in him made this the easiest decision in her life. She didn't have to wait for him to take her in his arms again before she said as clearly and lovingly as possible, "Yes, Vic. Anything you want, my darling."

CHAPTER EIGHT

The cellars were squirming like a beehive. Too much so, Vic realized, noticing the way people were running around in circles, bumping into each other, creating nothing but well-meaning chaos. He silently helped Laura down the treacherous steps, and they remained at the entrance to the cellars, her hand clasped tightly in his, while he calmly surveyed the hubbub. She saw the frown clouding the handsome face she loved so much, and pressing close to him, she whispered in his ear, "I'm afraid things are a bit frantic, aren't they?"

He nodded honestly. "Sure, but don't worry about it." He didn't know most of the people buzzing about, and nobody could really see him because of the shadows. Most of the light came from single electric bulbs hanging from the high rafters. Like everything else in this venerable place, the lighting was outmoded and almost useless. He could see Matt and Tina in the half-light by the row of casks housing the precious vintage. Their heads were close together, their faces lined with tension and worry. Next to them hovered Bill Hoyt, just as anxious. Unfortunately, it was Lucy Kaye, improbably hauling around wooden trestles to be used as improvised worktables, who first spotted Vic. "Hey, I must be seeing things!" she bellowed, instantly capturing the complete attention of everyone in the room. "Laura, luv, is that Vic Remo standing over there with you?"

"Yes, it is." Laura lifted her chin and looked across to where Matt was standing too quietly. His usual inscrutable air had vanished, and he stared at Laura and then Vic with open rebellion in his eye.

Dropping Laura's hand, Vic advanced into the room. "We always seem to meet in the strangest places, don't we, Lucy." He smiled warmly at the dumpy little woman. "Like opera, I suspect you don't know a darned thing about wine, either. Correct me if I'm wrong."

"You're dead right," she agreed, without a trace of shame. "For me, wine either tastes good or it doesn't, and that's all I know about it. But a sensitive palate isn't a prerequisite for lending a hand around here, you know." She squinted and cocked her head to the side. "I've come to help Laura any way I can. Why are you here?"

"Maybe for the same reason." He looked at Laura. "Let's go over to the casks."

The noise and commotion seemed to lessen as Vic and Laura neared the spot where Matt and Tina were standing. Lucy let the wooden plank she had been wrestling with fall loudly to the stone floor and followed to join the nervous group. Nobody said anything at first, but Matt finally asked Laura, "What's he doing here?"

"I asked Vic to come."

"Why?" Matt didn't hide the fact that he thought Laura

had committed an act of treachery. Tina, however, was prepared to give Vic the benefit of the doubt and smiled at him encouragingly.

It was Vic who answered. "Maybe like everybody else here, Matt, I've come to help save a special vintage." He turned to look at Bill Hoyt. "That's why you're here, isn't it?"

"You've got it," Bill said, meeting Vic's eye squarely.

"Good," Vic said quietly. "Now that we all understand each other's motives, I suggest . . ."

But Matt still balked. "Well, I don't understand."

Laura realized it was time to appeal to Matt's common sense. "We have to stop wasting time! Vic will take a test of the wine to decide if it's ready—"

"We don't need any more tests!" Matt said, stung. "Laura, you know Bill and I have already—!"

"Stop it, Matt. I didn't mind when you called Bill in to give advice, did I? We have to be careful, and we have to be *sure*."

Vic waited patiently for Matt to simmer down. It took a nod from Bill, but Matt finally conceded. By now, Vic had everybody's attention. "I'll need some data from you, Matt. You, too, Bill."

They congregated around a massive cask that stood in the middle of the row. The thick stone walls and slate floors amplified every spoken word. Feet shuffled in tension. Their faces were caught in the shafts of dim light. Vic smiled quickly and reassuringly at Laura with a message meant only for her eyes. Tina stuck close to Matt, and Bill Hoyt looked frankly relieved now that Vic had taken command. Old Beppo watched Vic like a hawk. Lucy was thoroughly confused, but she egged Vic on with a wide wink. All eyes were riveted on him.

The next few minutes were spent in a terse three-way conversation among Vic, Matt, and Bill. To Lucy's ears it sounded like a language spoken by moon dwellers. Vic was asking all the questions. "What did you think of the texture this morning, Bill?"

"A beautiful color and crystal clear."

"Matt, was the last racking done with bentonite?"

"Yes, all of them were from the very first."

"When was the final collage finished?"

"About twenty-four hours ago."

"That's not good enough," Vic said, with a slight snap to his words. "I don't want to know *about*, I want to know *exactly!*"

When Matt answered, it was in a very firm voice. "Exactly twenty-four hours ago."

"Good," Vic murmured, returning Laura's squeeze. "No filteration to take out the sediment, right?"

"No," Matt answered, with a lilt of pride. "We've never done it that cheap way at *this* Winery."

Vic let that snide comment pass. "What about the bouquet? Is it full and fragrant? Has the dryness balanced with the vanilla? Does the tang of acid roll into a long, leisurely finish?"

For the first time, Matt hesitated. "I . . . well, to my nose, it was magnificent. But . . ." He glanced at Bill Hoyt for support.

"Don't look at me," Bill said, shaking his head. "I can balance any chemistry you want in the labs, but when it comes down to aesthetics, I leave that to experts like Vic."

"Then there's only one way to tell." He exuded such calm self-assurance that even Lucy, who was completely lost, strained to hear his every word. "The final judgment is in the glass, isn't it? Tina, would you please get me two glasses?"

She hurried over to the cabinet where the Baccarat stemware was kept for this ritual. Returning in an instant, she handed Vic both crystal glasses with more than respect in her eyes; there was excitement, too. Vic nodded his thanks and then gave one of the glasses to Laura. "We'll make the test together." He turned to the massive cask and removed the bung very carefully. Then he withdrew a small amount of the wine with a thief. Pouring only about an inch of the golden liquid to each glass, he whispered to Laura, "Tell me what you think."

She took the glass in her two hands and held it lovingly, cherishing the moment as long as possible. She had helped her father with this ritual many times, always with a tiny twinge of fear that the wine would not be perfect. Then she would be filled with joy when her father pronounced the wine to be brilliant. Now she was sharing this wonderful custom with Vic, too.

She placed the glass against her lips, remembering the last time they had sipped wine from the same glasses. How she would have felt if she had never seen him again! She tasted the wine.

Vic's voice broke through the silence that had taken hold of the room. "Laura?"

"It's the finest D'Asti I've ever tasted." All of her knowledge and experience seemed to be in that remark, but she chose to leave him the final opinion. "Darling?"

Everybody crowded a little closer to the massive cask, breathlessly awaiting Vic's judgment. He didn't dally, quickly sipping a tiny amount of the wine. He let the liquid trickle slowly down his throat, drop by drop. Unexpectedly, it was Matt who couldn't bear the strain anymore. He pleaded, "For God's sake, tell us!"

"Supremely brilliant." There was a touch of awe in this. "I would say it's superior to *L'occhio del falcone,* and it would be a crime against mankind not to preserve it right now!"

In the jubilant uproar that followed, Vic pulled Laura tightly to his side. He turned and held out his hand. "Matt, my compliments. You did one hell of a job!" He also included Bill Hoyt in his smile of congratulations.

Old Beppo was dancing a jolly jig with Lucy of all people, and he insisted he had known all along the wine would be perfect at this moment. "The moon is full, the wind is blowing from the north, and the weather is clear!" he shouted, reciting the old belief that only under these conditions could an extraordinary wine be produced.

Vic allowed everybody to blow off steam for a little while longer, then he called for silence. "Now comes the hard part." He had climbed on one of the cask's supporting rigs so that everyone could hear him. "I intend to save *all* the wine, and this is how we're going to do it."

The night had turned into another day, but Laura hadn't left the cellars. Neither had Vic. Although he had ordered groups of twenty people to work no longer than three hours at a time, and each shift was replenished with new and rested volunteers, he had not been able to order Laura around. "I'll rest when you rest," she had said stubbornly, adding a swift kiss to soften his resistance. He had relented only when she had consented to a more leisurely kiss. Both were oblivious of the people around them. After that, matters settled down to a more mundane, backbreaking routine.

Laura's first worry had been how to feed so many people for at least two days. Lucy, however, had anticipated this particular predicament and found a stopgap solution. Giorgio, looking very strange in casual work clothes instead of his usual impeccable chauffeur's garb, soon appeared laden with picnic baskets bursting with food furnished by the Vallejo House. When that was finished, the farmers began coming to work armed with huge earthenware dishes filled with their wives' choicest Italian specialities. They proudly brought bottles of their own wine, too. A mandolin and even an accordion appeared to lend a festive air to the serious work. Vic had removed every piece of unnecessary furniture so that an unobstructed assembly line could be set up where each worker had an assigned task. The furniture was put to use on the lawns so that everybody could eat and rest.

The bone-crushing work was beginning to wear Laura down, and she broke off for a few hours sleep. She threw herself on her bed, determined to sleep only two or three hours. When she awoke, feeling stupefied and numb, the sun had already set. She realized in horror that she had slept away most of the afternoon. Rushing through her shower, she threw on the first pair of jeans she could find, pulled on an old, comfortable shirt, and then ran as fast as her bare feet would carry her out of her room. Walking carefully by Donna Evangelina's door, Laura wondered what the woman could possibly be doing locked in her room so long. She hadn't seen her mother-in-law since yesterday, but Tina had told her that Donna Evangelina had been phoning all over northern California since early this morning. Laura wondered why only for a moment; she had too many other things on her mind to worry about Donna Evangelina's plots.

Back in the cellars, she spotted Matt immediately. He was checking the growing stacks of crates that were resting against the stone walls. Each crate contained nine dark bottles that had been specially ordered by Andrea D'Asti years ago to hold this vintage. Working along with Matt, Tina was meticulously marking each bottle with white ink and then adding a corresponding number in a large black ledger. "Matt, where's Vic?" Laura asked.

"Over there." He smiled, pointing to the corner of the cellars. "I wouldn't say he fell asleep, collapsed is a better way to put it. Don't worry," he said, seeing Laura's startled face. "He's fine."

"I must say, sis, you look much better," Tina said, fresh as a daisy herself. "Matt and I took turns resting, and I sent Lucy and Giorgio home. They were both bushed!"

"Thanks, honey. You, too, Matt. Thanks so much!" Laura crossed the room, talking and joking with the farmers she had known all her life. They were giving so much of their time and love to this project. When she finally knelt down by Vic's motionless body, all she could see was the top of his head and one arm that had fallen out from under a rough blanket someone had compassionately thrown over him. She pulled the blanket gently away from his face. He looked so tired! With one arm curled under his head, he seemed oblivious of everything. She couldn't help it, she was compelled to touch the dark hair just once, letting the jet locks coil like dusky silk around her fingers. Positive that one tiny kiss wouldn't disturb his sleep, she had barely brushed her lips against his when his eyes opened. "Oh, darling, I'm so sorry!" she whispered. "I didn't mean to wake you."

He slowly closed his eyes again. He didn't look the least bit angry. "Tell you what, Laura. Do that again, only don't be so gentle. I think this blanket can cover both of us."

"Wouldn't that be something?" She laughed, wiggling free from the strong circle his arms made. "We would certainly create the juiciest scandal to rock Sonoma in years!"

He was suddenly wide awake. Sitting up, he glanced at his watch. "I've been asleep for hours."

"Please get some more rest," she begged, standing up. "Matt told me you practically collapsed."

He rose to his feet. "I've never collapsed in my life." He reached to hug her again, and then he rubbed his hand across his face. "Do you think Matt has a spare razor around?"

She started to nod, but had to stop immediately when his mouth came crushing down on her lips regardless of the scandal it would create up and down the length of Sonoma.

The work continued. The crates now covered two entire walls. Lucy and Giorgio returned, and they took turns relieving anybody who needed rest or food. By the afternoon of the second day, Laura began to realize that they were very close to accomplishing a miracle. "No," she thought, "Vic has accomplished a miracle!" He was constantly in the center of things, advising, commanding, even inspiring. When the situation demanded, he was ready with a funny story to lighten the mood or to bring a broad smile to a tired face. There seemed to be no task he would not or could not do if the need arose. Whatever resentment or distrust anybody had felt toward him at the beginning had totally evaporated. Bill Hoyt and Matt kept pace in complete harmony.

The sun had just met the horizon, and the late afternoon

breezes rustled across the ground. It was the most wonderful part of the day. Laura was glad she had stepped outside to catch the lovely moment. She breathed deeply and stretched until she tingled all over.

"I don't know which is lovelier, you or that sunset."

"Ah, Vic, I'm so happy you decided to take a breather, too."

They strolled along silently, just delighted to be with one another. He slipped his arm around her shoulder. They passed the farmers and smiled, listening to their *canzoni* and the plaintive sound of their music. "I've forgotten to ask you about the contract. Did you bring it with you, Vic?"

"Yes, I have it in the car. Let's walk over there so you can read the contents for yourself," he suggested.

"All right, but I hate reading legal rigmarole. Why don't you tell me all about it yourself?"

So he sketched out the wonderful concessions he had wrung from Canova. She hugged him, especially when she heard she could keep the house. "Thank you, darling. Oh, I love you so much!" She meant every word of it, too. Suddenly, a large van pulled up to the mansion. "What on earth can that be?" They quickly walked over to get a better look at the vehicle. Once she was close enough to read the business sign painted on the van's door, Laura gasped in surprise. Very tastefully and artistically, the sign read Spandoni Bakery, Sacramento.

"I didn't know your husband had other relatives besides his mother," Vic said.

"Yes, the Spandonis are a very large family," she murmured, thoroughly puzzled. "But I've never met any of them, and I didn't expect a visit."

The enigma was solved when Donna Evangelina

swooped out the front door of the mansion and charged down the stairs like a war galleon in full sail, looking neither left or right, a bulging suitcase under each arm. She had settled herself like a rock in the van's front seat and the vehicle had raced off before Laura realized what had happened. "Oh, no! I can't let her go just like that. . . ."

"Laura, honey, take it easy. Maybe it's the best thing that could happen."

"I was rude to her," she tried to explain, feeling very guilty. "And now I've driven her out of the house."

He knew the situation had to be resolved immediately. Laura had too much on her mind to be bothered with Donna Evangelina's peevish selfishness. "Nobody can *drive* your mother-in-law to do anything she doesn't want. Be sensible, won't you? What's wrong with her living with another relative, anyway? I'm sure she'll be very comfortable."

"I'm not sure it's right, that's all."

"Why must you bear the burden of keeping her? Especially since she has her own relatives. You've done more than enough for her. Anyway, I thought you told me all the ghosts were gone, darling."

That did it. "They're all gone, Vic. I swear it."

"Prove it to me then. Forget about everything else and think only about us."

"All right, I'll try." She couldn't resist his pleas. She really couldn't deny him anything! "Let's get the contract."

The car was still parked where he had abandoned it two days ago. He took the contract out of the glove compartment and gave it to Laura. She glanced at it briefly, refolded it, and then tucked it under her arm. "I'll tell everyone just as soon as we've finished bottling the wine."

Matt's shout rang out loud and clear. They rushed back to the old buildings and found him almost glowing with excitement. "Come on back to the cellars, you two! All the wine has been bottled!"

Laura could hardly believe it. Even after they had entered the large room and saw Tina marking the last bottle, Laura could still hardly believe it. "Darling," she whispered to Vic, "I'll never be able to thank you, you know that."

"Give me some time, and I'll think of a way," he said, smiling.

Everybody congratulated Laura and praised Vic. She knew this was the right time to tell Tina, her workers, and her friends about the change of management. "Listen to me, everybody!" She went on to tell them that she had promised to sell the Winery to Canova and that Vic had worked out a wonderful contract that ensured that everybody would keep their jobs and that the Winery would always bear the D'Asti name. When she finished, a little breathless and flushed, she was confronted with a stunned silence. What was the matter? she wondered. Didn't they understand that this was the only way she could save the Winery? She searched for Vic's hand, found it, and felt the response she needed to give her strength and courage. It was Lucy who first had the nerve to speak up. "I'm not family, and I don't work here, but I'm your friend, luv, and I think it's a great idea. If anybody really cares about *you*, then they'll realize you did the right thing!"

Matt looked as if he had been hit by a thunderbolt. He was literally speechless. Tina gazed at Laura and then took another good look at Matt. Without further hesitation, she walked up to her sister and gave her a hug and a big kiss on the cheek. "I agree with Lucy and Vic. You're the one who has had to sacrifice and worry, and anybody who doesn't realize you deserve to have a little fun out of life, well... he's an insensitive louse, that's all!" She glared at Matt.

Laura felt her heart constrict; she knew what price her sister might have to pay for her loyalty. "Tina—!"

"The only thing we have left to do is label all those bottles," Tina interrupted, trying to be practical. "Papa had chosen a very special stock to print labels for this wine. Do you still have it, Laura?"

"Yes, I saved it." She began to pull herself together, but she was still chilled by the hostility she felt around her. "We might even use a reproduction of the old tasting room to commemorate this vintage. Vic has talked me into reopening the room to the public."

"Oh, sis, that's wonderful." Tina swore she would never speak to Matt again! How could he be so mean?

Over the past two years, Lucy had painfully pieced together most of the details of what had taken place in the tasting room, and she knew that Vic had to be responsible for the change in Laura. After giving Vic a silent salute, she turned to Laura. "Tell you what, luv. I just happen to have the finest lithographer in California working on my newspaper. Why don't you let him do the artwork, and I'll print all the labels for you, nice and fancy. Okay? That will be my gift to you for being such a great gal."

It was such a fantastically generous gift that Laura searched for words to thank her friend. Finding none, she threw her arms around Lucy and squeezed with all her might. It would have been a beautiful moment, but Bill Hoyt shattered it and her life with only a few sentences.

"If you sign that contract you're holding in your hand, Miss D'Asti, then you won't be needing those labels."

"What do you mean?"

"Once that contract is signed those bottles will be on their way to Ricardo Canova's main plant. In an hour, every one of them will be bearing the Canova Gold label, believe me!"

"Oh, no, Bill." She smiled, the only person in the room who didn't grasp the full implications of what he had just said. "You don't understand. The contract stipulates that *all* the wine produced by this Winery will bear the D'Asti label."

"I know what I'm talking about," Bill said, his voice gruff and apologetic at the same time. "I've seen it happen to other winegrowers who have sold out to Canova. Sure, the contract may say the original name will be maintained, but Canova has big-time lawyers working for him, and he can afford to break any rules he wants. Nobody's ever won a court fight against Canova! If he's hot for a certain vintage, he'll slap his own private label on it, and he'll get away with it!"

"It's true!" yelled one of the farmers. Another shouted out, "Yes, he did the same thing to me!" As the growing anger circled the room, Lucy tried to buffer the shock Laura would soon be feeling by holding her friend as protectively as possible. Even old Beppo was openly rebeling. He raised his fist and swore, "I won't work for Canova! Nobody can force me to work for a thief, *per un ladro!*"

It was inevitable that Matt Moyer would find his tongue sooner or later, and when he did he gave voice to the one thought no one had dared speak aloud. "Remo, you've known all along this would happen, haven't you?"

"You're crazy," Vic snapped. "I don't know what was

stipulated in those other contracts, but I know what's in Laura's contract because I wrote it. And I'll see that it's honored!"

"I don't believe you! I think you worked like a dog to get this vintage bottled for Canova, not for Laura." Matt looked anything but mild now. "All you've ever wanted is that wine—for your boss!" There was a strange look in his sandy eyes. "It's either that, or Canova's really suckered you!"

Both men instinctively moved toward one another. Tina, wretched and perplexed, was certain of only one thing: If Vic was provoked any further and lost that iron self-control, he was quite capable of smashing Matt to a pulp with one furious slash of his fist. And although she was lividly angry with him, she really didn't want anything drastic to happen to Matt. "Why don't you stop this!" she cried, hanging on to Matt's arm. "Can't you see how you're upsetting Laura? All this yelling and threatening and shouting isn't going to prove anything, is it?"

Vic couldn't see Laura's face because it was crushed against Lucy's shoulder, but Tina's common sense cleared his head. "I'll get you all the proof you need!"

When Laura looked up, he was gone. "Where did he go?"

"To have it out with Canova, I'm sure." Lucy was ready to burst into tears, but this didn't even register in Laura's mind. *Vic.* Nothing mattered to her at this moment but Vic. "Wait! Please wait, darling! I want to go with you!"

Laura had only one desire—to be with Vic, to protect him, and to stop him from hurting anybody else. "I love you, and I know you wouldn't hurt me in any way! I believe you! Please, darling . . ."

But the car continued to hurtle toward San Francisco at a blinding speed. Laura stared at Vic's profile. His mouth was tight and cold, so cold that not one word would come out of those lips. He wouldn't or couldn't hear her. Her nervousness and fear grew the closer they got to the bay. He seemed hellbent to get to Canova fast. The high, shrill sound of the screeching tires pierced her head as the car took sharp turns and reached even higher speeds on the straightaways. Finally Vic was forced to slow down when they crossed the bridge. He came to a complete stop at the toll booth, but only for a second. Though he had given the guard a large bill, he didn't bother to wait for the change before hitting the accelerator again. The main stream of traffic headed for the Marina, but he cut across to catch the shortcut through the Presidio. Branches of pines and eucalyptus trees—alarming forms in the darkness—scraped against the windows. The tortuous road ended at the stone gates that marked the exit from the Army base. One more block and they were at the pinnacle of Pacific Heights, the private reserve of the city's very rich.

The massive iron gates of the Canova home stood open, and Vic stopped at the top of the curved flagstone driveway. The three-story mansion, standing higher than any of its neighbors, loomed behind Vic as he opened Laura's door and pulled her from the car. Clutching her hand like steel, he silently rushed up the gray stone steps fronting the majestic house. Warned of their arrival by the roar of Vic's car, a butler swung open the double oak doors just as they arrived at the top step. "Good evening, Mr. Remo." He stood aside to let them pass into the anteroom. "Mr. Canova is in the library, but I don't think he was expecting you." His eyes rapidly flicked over **Laura** and then returned to Vic, "Shall I announce you, sir?"

"Don't bother."

Leaving the butler still standing uncertainly at the **door**, Vic turned down a wing of the palatial home, dragging Laura along. Their footsteps rang out on the marble floors that covered the entire length of a hallway. A garden in full bloom could be seen through tall French windows. The collection of priceless Canova oil paintings covered the opposite wall.

Before he opened the door at the end of the corridor, Vic took hold of the contract Laura still clutched in her hands. "Please, Vic, I don't want to see Canova, I don't want to go in there. Can't we forget all this? I believe you! Can't we just go away and forget—?"

"No, we can't. *I can't!*"

In a deep silence far more terrifying than a scream, they entered the library. The room was long and high, and the view of the bay from its cut-glass windows was almost staggering. With cool blue walls, inlaid parquet floors, and very little furniture, the library encouraged the visitor's eye to dwell on its treasures: the priceless fifteenth century manuscripts and the awesome collection of medieval Flemish madonnas. At the end of the room, Ricardo Canova was standing by a beautiful Empire desk, deeply involved in a piece of paper he held unsteadily in his hand. Whether or not he noticed them was unclear. All he said was, "Bill Hoyt!"

Vic touched Laura's hand in warning, and she quickly swallowed the gasp that had almost escaped from her mouth. They remained close to the windows, dwarfed by the size of the room. She marveled at the way Vic controlled his temper. Canova seemed to be obsssessed. "Bill

Hoyt! She's gone back to him. Carole, I mean." He slammed the piece of paper down on his desk. "She gave this note to the butler and just left the house about a half hour ago. No luggage, no jewelry, nothing!" His mouth looked grim as he shook his head in disbelief. "I thought I had destroyed that relationship years ago. But all of a sudden, three husbands later, she decides she still loves her first husband!" He still didn't seem to be completely aware of their presence. "I needed her beauty in this house so much when her mother left me. I still need her . . ." Canova's head snapped back. "I'm sorry, I was preoccupied." Laura could almost see him filing away whatever emotions he was feeling until he had the time and inclination to deal with them, just like a human computer! He immediately became cool and attentive. "I'm very surprised to see you here, Miss D'Asti, but welcome! May I get you a drink?"

"No, thank you." She would choke before she would accept anything from him.

"No? Well, at least sit down, won't you?"

Her knees felt as if they would give way any moment, and she sank into a nearby chair. So that's what Bill Hoyt had meant when he said that he had an old score to settle with this man! Carole and Bill had once been married. Did Vic know that? It didn't matter. Laura irrationally wished Carole and Bill would find some happiness again, and her reasons were not entirely selfish, either. But Vic and Canova were talking, and she had to hear every word, no matter how devastating.

"I'm glad to see you, too, Vic, although I expected to hear from you yesterday."

"The D'Asti vintage peaked sooner than expected."

"What have you done about it?" There was a nervous edge to Canova's voice.

"It's been saved. We worked around the clock for forty-eight hours to save every last drop of it."

Frank admiration passed over Canova's dignified face. "Good! You must have worked like a maniac to get all that equipment in that Winery. A remarkable job!"

"We're all finished," Vic said very distinctly, not stopping to explain that none of Canova's equipment had been used, "except for the labeling."

"No problem, my friend. In fact, don't bother about the labels." He smiled mirthlessly.

"I like to finish any job I start, Canova, you know that."

"Yes, but this is different. I'll see to the labeling myself." His manner remained assured and untroubled. "I don't think I've told you, but I intend to put my own Canova Gold label on Andrea D'Asti's last vintage."

"That wasn't in the contract, was it?"

The tightness in Vic's voice made Canova look up, but he waved his hand as if to signify that this point was too unimportant to be discussed. "If you have one fault, Vic, it's that you're too honest," he said seriously. "To protect you from yourself, I was forced to keep you in the dark about this one thing. Oh, I've found a way to get around contracts in the past. No publicity, no court battles, just a lot of cash under the table. I'll honor every clause in the D'Asti contract—except the label on the vintage. That wine belongs to me."

Canova was beneath contempt! Laura couldn't bear to keep quiet any longer. "Why must my vintage be yours?"

"I don't really think you want to know the answer to that question, Miss D'Asti," he murmured, strolling to the window to gaze at the bay. "I don't really wish to hurt you, you know."

"No, not Laura," Vic said, beginning to understand the whole pathetic story. "It was Andrea D'Asti you wanted to hurt, wasn't it? Even though the poor man is dead."

"Let's just say I wanted to wipe away an insult." Canova continued to look at the lights below. "Miss D'Asti, did you know your father asked me for a large loan just before he died?"

"My father?" Impossible! "No, I didn't know. . . ."

Canova sighed. "Well, you may as well know everything. I'm sure he needed the money desperately or . . ."

"Or he wouldn't have lowered himself to come to you for the loan," Vic suggested sarcastically. Canova turned to look at him, suddenly puzzled. "As you said," Vic continued, "we may as well know the whole story. Go on."

Canova's gray eyes grew colder as he frowned. "Andrea D'Asti wanted to buy tractors and replace some worn-out pumps in the old buildings."

Vic's hand came down solidly on Laura's shoulder. Otherwise she couldn't have controlled her shaking. "Yes, we needed new pumps very badly . . . ."

"I think I offered him a very fair solution. I told him I would give him the money as a gift if he would use his influence and reputation to gain me the Amici Award. He laughed at me." He gazed out the window again. "When I again offered him the money as a gift if in addition he would *sell* me his new wine, which I knew would age magnificently, so that I could lay claim to the award, he laughed even louder. But," he said, not without a touch of pride, "the vintage was worth the wait." He allowed himself a short laugh. "I can assure you, my dear Miss D'Asti, this wine's fame will heal any wounds your father inflicted on me!"

"Why should you be allowed to ruin people's lives for an award that isn't even known outside the wine industry? It's not fair! You have everything anybody could want!" she cried bitterly, glancing around the beautiful room.

"I have *acquired* a great deal, my dear," he corrected, moving back to his desk. The words *respect* and *reputation* and *love* hung in the air as loudly as if they had been screamed in rage. "It's very hard for others to understand a man's secret passions." He saw the way Vic was holding Laura. "I had already guessed some of yours, Vic."

"You knew all about Laura's life when you deliberately sent me on this assignment that first day, didn't you?"

"Of course. It's worked out rather nicely for everybody, wouldn't you say? You obviously have Miss D'Asti's adoration, I have the vintage, and you, my friend, have a very large bonus coming to you. Now then, give me the contract."

Vic slowly came closer and tossed the white packet on the desk. He watched as Canova unhurriedly unfolded the sheets of paper and began to scan the bottom of each sheet. "You won't find what you're looking for," Vic murmured. "Laura never signed that contract. You don't own one inch of D'Asti land, and your label won't appear on one bottle of that vintage."

Canova's restraint was remarkable. He had just been denied something he had been lusting after for nearly four years, and yet he didn't flinch. "Why did you change your mind, Miss D'Asti? You've doomed the Winery, you know that, don't you?"

"I'd rather close the Winery forever than have anything

to do with you," Laura told him, standing and hurrying to Vic. "Thank God I found out the truth about you—and Vic did, too—before I signed that contract!"

"You know, I never thought you would do this to me, Vic." Canova's chiseled face looked pained. But then he shrugged. "It's a pity, really. A great winery and a fine career will go down the tubes at the same time, both for stupid, idiotic reasons."

"Aren't you being overly pessimistic?" Vic asked mockingly. "I'm not talking about my career; I was bound to find out about your illegal business methods sooner or later, and that would have been the end of our partnership anyway. You taught me to be ruthless, but I guess I would have eventually disappointed you with my honesty. No, I mean you're being too pessimistic about the Winery." His firm self-control finally deserted him, and his words were flecked with heat. "I've never worked as hard in my whole life as I have in the last two days, and yet I've never been happier! Whatever I accomplished, I did it without one cent of your dirty money and not one piece of your damned equipment! The Winery could be saved if somebody cared enough to invest the time and money to revive and organize it. What do you think, Laura?" He lifted her face so that their eyes locked. "I would like to try—on a permanant basis, of course."

"The only way I would consider such a proposal," she whispered, brushing her lips once, twice against his warm mouth, "would be on a permanant basis."

They were already halfway across the room when they heard, "How did you do it, Vic?" Canova remained standing at his desk, his back straight, his gaze like flint. "How did you manage to salvage all the vintage in such a short time without money or modern equipment?"

Vic's laugh sounded out of place in the emptiness of the majestic library. "Believe it or not, I did it with people. You'd be surprised by the different kinds of people that came from all over Napa-Sonoma to help. They didn't break their backs because of the D'Asti reputation, either. They did it simply out of a deep feeling of something they called *fratellanza*. Incidentally, Canova, that means friendship." Laura might have added that it meant *love*, too, but Vic's mocking words were enough, she knew.

CHAPTER NINE

Every night since she had married Vic almost a year ago, Laura went to sleep in her husband's arms, never knowing if an unexpected crisis would crop up in the vineyards, interrupting their precious private time. Sometimes the phone rang in the middle of the night, instantly waking both of them. Sometimes the summons came at dawn with a discreet knock on their bedroom door, waking only Vic. When this happened, he would leave noiselessly, lovingly, gently, letting her sleep on until morning. The late summer had been kind to them, with just enough rain and not too much harsh sunshine, allowing the vendange to prosper on the vine and permitting them the luxury every now and then of an entire night to themselves. Last night had been such a night, and Laura had slept late on purpose. Today was a holiday, a wonderful, do-nothing, happy holiday! She stretched and rolled over on her side, loathing the idea of getting out of bed. Where was Vic? she wondered for a moment. Ah, yes! He had left for his regular morning field inspection. She wished he hadn't left her, not on this wonderful, special morning!

"Laura! Are you going to sleep all day? Get up!"

Tina's laughing voice was coming from somewhere down on the veranda. Laura slipped out of bed and put on a bright, thin robe. The bedroom windows were wide open, and the sunshine splashed into the room, flooding it with a gaiety that matched her mood. "Good morning! What are you doing up so early?" she asked, bending over the windowsill and looking down at Tina.

"It's not that early! Come on down. We'll have breakfast here on the veranda. It's such a beautiful day," Tina said, shading her eyes from the sun.

"It is!" Laura looked out over the vineyards, lush and green, hoping to catch a glimpse of Vic driving around the fields. But she couldn't spot him. "I'll get dressed and be right down, Tina."

The first thing she saw when she walked out on the veranda was a charmingly set table and their mother's delicate china. "I really think we should use Mama's chocolate set more often," Tina said. "Anyway, today we're having a guest for breakfast."

"Of course, Lucy! I'm so happy you asked her to join us this morning. When did she say she'd be here?"

"Are you kidding? She's been here with her army of ranch hands practically since the crack of dawn! Oh, Laura, she's decorating the gardens so beautifully for tonight's supper party!"

"I don't know how I can ever thank her enough." Laura felt suddenly chagrined and a slow, revealing blush crept up to cover her face. "I should be ashamed of myself. While everybody else has been busy at work around here, I've been sleeping the morning away."

"And what about the mornings when the rest of us are snoozing in our warm beds and you and Vic have been slaving out in the fields before the sun is up? Honestly, Laura!"

She smiled at Tina. A look full of warmth and affection passed between the two sisters. "I agree with you about this china," she said, pouring both of them some hot chocolate. "We should use it more often. Every day if you like, Tina."

"Because every day has been rather special since you married Vic?" Tina teased.

Laura nodded. "That's exactly what I mean." A shaft of sunshine fell across the engagement diamond on her sister's hand, turning the facets into a riot of sparkles. "How is the new house coming along?"

"Fine! Matt promises to have it finished before the wedding. Ah, sis, I still can't believe all that land really belongs to us."

Laura had given Tina and Matt a large acreage on the northern end of the vineyards as a wedding present, and Matt was supervising the building of a lovely home where Tina and he would live after their wedding next month. "I hate to sound like an older, more experienced woman" —Laura laughed—"but I hope and pray you will be as happy with Matt as I've been with Vic."

"Now, don't you two look as pretty as a picture sitting up there on the old veranda," whooped Lucy, struggling up the stairs. "Whew! Do I need a cup of coffee."

Laura jumped away from the table to hug her friend. "Sure you won't have some Italian chocolate, instead? It's really delicious."

"Heck, no," Lucy said, glancing at the rich, exotic brew with naked distrust. "I don't know how you gals can stomach that stuff." She gratefully accepted a cup of honest black coffee from Tina, took a huge gulp, sat down, and immediately took off her shoes. "Ah, that's much better."

"Let me get you some breakfast. After all, that's the least I can do to thank you for decorating the gardens for the Amici Awards supper tonight." Laura filled a plate with all the delicacies Tina had turned out for a real *prima colazione*—with California variations, of course. "Thank you so much for everything."

"My pleasure, luv. Anyway, I'm putting out all this effort for purely selfish reasons, you know that."

"Your idea of combining the Amici Awards *and* a charity drive for your favorite projects was an absolute stroke of genius," Tina admitted, grinning.

"And don't think I won't lean heavy on those old geezers for lots of bucks, either!" She winked broadly at the sisters. "Speaking of old geezers, what ever happened to Donna Evangelina?"

"She's quite comfortable living in Sacramento with her family," Laura said, not feeling any of the old guilt.

"Good riddance." Tina sniffed.

"Stop making faces, Laura. I agree!" Lucy leaned across the table. "Good riddance to Carole Canova, too. Seems things are okay between her and Bill Hoyt. Last word I've had is that they've bought a vineyard in Upstate New York. Imagine Carole getting her hands soiled with good, honest dirt!"

Laura wondered if Lucy knew that she really didn't care about anybody other than those she loved. As she sat having breakfast with her sister and her best friend, surrounded by the vineyards and the comfortable beauty of the old mansion, she reflected on the irony of her life: Vic had urged her to be selfish and indulgent, and yet he had become the center of her entire world. Did Lucy really understand this remarkable fact?

Lucy certainly did understand. "You and Vic have created a miracle," said Lucy, taking another swig of coffee and wisely changing the subject. "Every time I come here, I'm astounded by what all of you have done to this place. A year ago, this Winery was doomed. Now look at it! You've doubled your production, and you've maintained all the D'Asti quality. Last year's supreme vintage is the talk of the wine world, too. By the way, where is Vic?"

Laura had been wondering the same thing. "He should be along any moment now. Oh, I think I see him."

The road leading in from the fields was hidden from their view by the dense vines, but telltale puffs of dust signaled that someone was driving down that road in a big hurry. In a few minutes, Vic brought a snazzy Jeep to a halt directly in front of the house. He wasn't alone, either. Bella popped out of the Jeep, letting go a bunch of hysterical barks.

"Don't tell me that high-class mutt has turned traitor?" Lucy said, amazed to see the dog fawning all over Vic as he waved and smiled in their direction.

"No, Bella just has enough love to share between us." Laura smiled at the dog's antics. "But I have to admit she's gone off the deep end over Vic. She follows him everywhere!"

Vic came running up the steps with Bella right at his heels. "Lucy, you're sexier than ever!"

"Hey! I'm happy to know the country life hasn't robbed you of your San Francisco charm," Lucy yelped, catching him in a big bear hug. Damn! He got handsomer every day, she realized. He was deeply tanned from long hours in the fields, and the few added strands of silver at the temples in his otherwise jet-black hair only added more mystery to his striking, sensual looks. The way he gazed at Laura after casually wiping his brow on his denim shirt sleeve told Lucy all she had to know about the source of his not-too-subtle air of total male contentment. Ah, love, Lucy thought.

"Hello, honey," he said, bending his lean body and kissing Laura quickly. With a snap of his fingers he put an end to Bella's shenanigans. The little creature immediately plopped down under the table. Glancing over to where Tina was sitting, he said, "Matt seems to be in a muddle about a few things out there! He's having problems with the interior of the new house. I think a little tender loving care and a lot of female advice would help."

"Tina to the rescue." She laughed. "See you tonight!" She blew everyone a good-bye kiss and ran off.

"I suppose Matt is just as loony in love," Lucy stated, squinting after Tina.

"Oh, yes. The poor man is befuddled and bewitched. He never had a chance against my sister, you know. Tina's been in love with him since she was a teen-ager." Laura sighed contently. "How about some breakfast, Vic?"

"Sounds great, honey. But if you don't mind, none of the chocolate stuff. I'll just help myself to some coffee." Vic peered into Lucy's cup. "I'm glad to see I'm not the only one around here who can't swallow that brew."

"It does my old heart good to know Laura hasn't vamped you into giving up all your bachelor habits." Lucy smirked and then pointed to the driveway in front of the house. "What did you do, Vic? Trade in your spectacular Italian torpedo for that Jeep?"

"Not on your life!" He took a laden plate from Laura

and set it on the table. Then he pulled his wife down on his lap. "We keep the car in the city."

"Smart idea, not giving up the apartment in San Francisco. It's the perfect romantic nest to run away to once in a while, eh?"

"Not as much as we'd like, Lucy," Laura said, brushing her lips against a wisp of Vic's hair that was fluttering in the breeze. "However, we plan to spend all next week at Vic's apartment—oh, I mean *our* apartment! It's the beginning of the opera season, you know."

Lucy moaned. "I can't put myself through that torture one more time. I won't be there. But we can have lunch together, okay?"

"Yes, that would be lovely." Laura had enjoyed feeling Vic's hair against her lips so much that now she continued to move her mouth down the side of his brow to the top of his cheekbone. "Right after the opera, we leave on our belated honeymoon for Sicily so that I can meet Vic's parents. It'll be our first wedding anniversary."

"And then you come back for the wedding!" Lucy had the distinct impression neither Vic nor Laura was really paying much attention to anything she was saying.

Laura did murmur, "Yes, Tina's wedding . . ." Vic had reacted with a swift spasm when Laura had first begun to kiss his hair. He was now involved in slowly tracing a line against her throat with his full mouth.

"Tell you what, folks," Lucy said quickly. "I still have a lot of work to do." She put on her shoes and wriggled away from the table. "I'll see you later." She fled down the stairs, knowing that it was quite impossible for either of them to answer.

Possibly five minutes later, Laura finally broke away

from Vic long enough to whisper, "I think we shocked Lucy."

"You've got to be kidding. Nothing shocks Lucy."

"But somebody else might pass by. Not everybody is as broad-minded as Lucy, you know."

"You might be right," he murmured. "Let's go upstairs."

"Darling, I just got out of bed . . . ."

"What the hell does that have to do with it?"

She agreed; that was definitely a very poor excuse!

Just before the guests were due to arrive, Laura went by herself to look at the gardens by moonlight. Lucy had created a wonderland on the sprawling, lush lawns. Intimate tables had been decorated with candles encased in delicate crystal lamps to protect the fragile flames from the breeze. White roses abounded everywhere, their fragrance mingling with the sweet evening air. The night was as lovely as any she could recall in the Valley of the Moon.

"You're beautiful."

She turned to look at Vic and saw that he was aware of her tiny touch of romanticism. She had deliberately chosen to wear white, the same color she had worn at last year's Amici Awards ceremony. This time, however, her gown was formal and elegant. It touched the ground with swirls of chiffon. Much more importantly, this time Vic was a part of her very being. Now he was her husband and lover, not her enemy. "You look wonderful yourself," she said admiringly, giving in to the totally feminine impulse to reach out and smooth an imaginary crease on the sleeve of his dinner jacket and straighten a black tie that had been already knotted to perfection.

"Our guests are beginning to arrive, Laura."

They strolled back to the house hand in hand. As they neared the front steps of the gracious old mansion, they could see the first limousines beginning to approach the road that ended at the arbor. They would have only a few more precious moments alone together, and Laura needed desperately to ask him something, something she had just realized.

Always sensitive to her moods, Vic wanted to know, "What is it, darling?"

"For the first time tonight you feel as if you really *belong* here, don't you?"

He didn't answer the question immediately, but he knew exactly what she meant. The grapes on the vines, perfect and succulent, would be his first harvest; then the young wine would be aged under his supervision; the vintage would be processed with machinery he had engineered and marketed with techniques he had pioneered. "Yes, I think I've earned that sense of belonging. We belong here together now."

They were to remember this moment for the rest of their lives. But, too quickly, it ended. Signor Angelotti, tottering more than ever but still young in spirit, was the first of many guests to be greeted by Laura and Vic. Lucy, who was co-hosting the party, joined them and greeted people, too. She was dressed in one of her more outrageous costumes of magenta plumes, and she was having the time of her life. Eventually, all the guests arrived and everyone sat down to supper. Tina and Matt were already seated when Vic led Laura to their table. Lucy stopped by on one of her scurrying rounds and beamed with approval at the two couples. "My, you people look nice! Tina, my pet, it should be against the law for any woman to look so pretty —and so young." She gave Tina's flowing pink silk gown a decided stamp of approval. But it was Matt, impeccably attired in black tie, who held her transfixed. "You look simply beautiful," she bellowed. "I would have never recognized you, Matt."

"Well, yes, thanks, Lucy," he muttered, his sandy eyes looking somewhat strained. People were turning around to stare and smile.

"Are you sure you don't need any help?" Laura interrupted before Lucy could shout out anything else that might really embarrass Matt. "You really have your hands full."

"No, thanks, luv. I'm having a ball!"

"How is your mercenary campaign coming along, old friend?" Vic asked, lowering his voice like a co-conspirator.

"Great! I've squeezed these old geezers—I mean these honorable gents—for a bundle of loot, don't worry. By the way, have you noticed that old Angelotti is being as mysterious about this year's award winner as he was about last year's recipient?"

"I think the little yearly drama he creates is what keeps him young. Don't spoil it for him, Lucy." Laura laughed.

"I won't, I promise. But who's scheduled to give the award?"

"I am," said Vic, "but I've already warned Angelotti I won't be giving a speech." He smiled a secret smile. "Like everyone else, I just want to hear who the winner is going to be."

"Well, we'll just have to wait and see. Have fun, everybody. Isn't this the most wonderful party?" Lucy staggered off, laughing and swearing as usual in a blur of magenta feathers.

The exquisite supper was served, accompanied by superb wines from the D'Asti private reserve. Vic poured wine from a bottle of the special vintage he had helped preserve halfway into the four glasses. Then he held up his own glass. "I think we should have a private family toast." The others, surprised and delighted, followed his example and held aloft their own glasses. "To Tina and Matt, *buona fortuna!* I'm sure Laura joins me in wishing you both all the happiness possible."

"With all my heart," Laura whispered. "Good luck!"

"Thank you," Matt told Vic and smiled warmly to include Laura. Tina, never at a loss for words, was much more exuberant. "Vic, Laura, you're both so wonderful! Here's a toast to both of you, and to the continued success of the D'Asti Winery!"

They drank to that, too. Laura spoke to Vic with her eyes, thanking him for the lovely gesture. When would this man cease to amaze her? she wondered. Never, she prayed, leaning back against the arm he had put around her shoulders. Tina's words had convinced her to do something she had been thinking about for some time. Seeing her face suddenly aglow with some happy thought, Vic raised his eyebrow. But the long, pleasurable supper had finally ended, and Signor Angelotti now commanded everybody's attention. The venerable gentleman stood very erect at the main table, his friendly, sparkling eyes full of glee. "Every year I find it much more difficult to stand for any length of time, so happily for you I will make my statement quite short!" He basked in the laughter that followed his little joke, and then he quickly glanced at the expectant faces before him. "I'm sure you'll remember that the Amici di Vino committee did a very daring thing last year, presenting the Amici Award to a newcomer to our ranks. He, in turn, rewarded our faith in his worthiness by then successfully preserving an extraordinary vintage, which otherwise might have been lost to us. Vic Remo, my dear boy! Would you please come up here and help me honor this year's recipient?"

To a chorus of applause, Vic worked his way around to Signor Angelotti and received the revered scroll into his own hands. He kept a sharp eye on the old gentleman too, because Signor Angelotti looked about to burst with excitement. "I spoke of an extraordinary wine a moment ago, and we all know the glory this wine has brought to our industry here in California." Signor Angelotti's voice grew stronger, not weaker. "Tonight, we honor tradition in the highest possible way—by again breaking tradition. We present this year's Amici di Vino Award for the first time to a woman—to Signora Lauretta Remo D'Asti!"

How long before dawn? Laura wondered, scanning the skies. Very soon now; a pale line of sunlight was just beginning to show on the horizon. The last guest had left hours ago, and the lawns had been cleared of all the tables and decorations. The Winery was at peace.

"You guessed I would win the award, didn't you?"

Vic smiled and handed Laura a glass of champagne. "How could you miss?" He drank some of the champagne, but kept his gaze firmly fixed on his beautiful wife. The twinkle in his dusky eyes didn't appear there by accident, either.

She had sipped some of the wine from her glass before she realized what she had done. "Oh, this is champagne!"

"You know, I never could understand why you don't like it?"

"I'll tell you a little secret. I *love* champagne, but it always makes me very tipsy, very fast!"

"You deserve to get a little tipsy tonight. Go on, drink it."

She did. "Oh, this tastes so good! See what you've done to me, darling." She laughed, running up the front steps of the mansion, the glass in one hand and the Amici scroll clasped in the other. Her delightful laughter brought Bella bounding out of the house, panting to join in the fun. Laura sat down on the top step, ignoring the damage she might be doing to her lovely gown. "You have been a very good dog all night." She scratched Bella's ears for a moment. Then absentmindedly finishing off the champagne, she discarded the glass and concentrated on unrolling the scroll. Ignored so soon, Bella scampered over to Vic, but he seemed to have other things on his mind too. The little creature glanced from master to mistress, and immediately took advantage of their obvious preoccupation. Like a shot, she raced into the semi-darkness. A squirrel had just caught her eye.

Meanwhile, Laura had been very seriously studying the way her name had been embossed on the scroll. "Signora Lauretta Remo D'Asti."

"You have the same look on your face that appeared when Tina offered her toast at the table. What are you thinking about, Laura?"

She gazed at him with a look that was dreamy, teasing, and serious all at the same time. "It has a very traditional ring to it, doesn't it? I mean the old-fashioned, Italian way of putting our two names together in that order. Mm-m-m, Remo D'Asti . . ."

"refer Mrs. Remo." He strolled up the stairs and sat tep below her. "Don't you?" While she pretended at very important question a great deal of thought, he pulled her face closer and took a long time lingering over her mouth before he let her speak again.

"That was a lovely kiss! Do it again, darling . . ." Finally, she pulled her head away and whispered, "I agree, I'll always insist on being called Mrs. Remo." Holding him very, very close, she said, "But from now on, this will be called the Remo-D'Asti Winery."

A while later, he said, "That's not necessary, you know that, darling . . ."

"It *is* necessary because you and you alone are responsible for bringing this Winery back to life. Oh, my darling, remember what you said? We really belong here, together."

"Laura . . ."

She put her fingers on his full, warm mouth, wanting no words of gratitude. "You really have to be gracious about this," she teased, "or I might be very tempted to tell everybody that my real name is Mrs. Vittorío Michelangelo Remo!"

"You wouldn't dare!"

"Oh?" The word hung in the air tauntingly. "Wouldn't I?" She let her hands slip along his broad shoulders until she stopped at the place where his dark skin gleamed against the white collar. His tie was still perfectly knotted. So slowly that it was almost deliciously tormenting, she pulled at one of the corners of the silk tie until it completely unraveled. Then, one by one, she undid the buttons of his shirt. "You should know by now, darling, that with you there is nothing I wouldn't dare!"

When You Want A Little More Than Romance—

Try A Candlelight Ecstasy!

Wherever paperback books are sold!

Bestsellers

- **NOBLE HOUSE** by James Clavell.............$5.95 (16483-4)
- **PAPER MONEY** by Adam Smith.................$3.95 (16891-0)
- **CATHEDRAL** by Nelson De Mille.................$3.95 (11620-1)
- **YANKEE** by Dana Fuller Ross......................$3.50 (19841-0)
- **LOVE, DAD** by Evan Hunter........................$3.95 (14998-3)
- **WILD WIND WESTWARD**
  by Vanessa Royal...$3.50 (19363-X)
- **A PERFECT STRANGER**
  by Danielle Steel...$3.50 (17221-7)
- **FEED YOUR KIDS RIGHT**
  by Lendon Smith, M.D. $3.50 (12706-8)
- **THE FOUNDING**
  by Cynthia Harrod-Eagles...............................$3.50 (12677-0)
- **GOODBYE, DARKNESS**
  by William Manchester...................................$3.95 (13110-3)
- **GENESIS** by W.A. Harbinson......................$3.50 (12832-3)
- **FAULT LINES** by James Carroll..................$3.50 (12436-0)
- **MORTAL FRIENDS** by James Carroll.........$3.95 (15790-0)
- **THE SOLID GOLD CIRCLE**
  by Sheila Schwartz..$3.50 (18156-9)
- **AMERICAN CAESAR**
  by William Manchester...................................$4.50 (10424-6)

At your local bookstore or use this handy coupon for ordering:

Dell DELL BOOKS
P.O. BOX 1000, PINE BROOK, N.J. 07058-1000

Please send me the books I have checked above. I am enclosing $_____ (please add 75c per copy to cover postage and handling). Send check or money order—no cash or C.O.D.'s. Please allow up to 8 weeks for shipment.

Mr./Mrs./Miss _____

Address _____

City_____ State/Zip _____

The unforgettable saga of a magnificent family
IN JOY AND IN SORROW
by JOAN JOSEPH

They were the wealthiest Jewish family in Portugal, masters of Europe's largest shipping empire. Forced to flee the scourge of the Inquisition that reduced their proud heritage to ashes, they crossed the ocean in a perilous voyage. Led by a courageous, beautiful woman, they would defy fate to seize a forbidden dream of love.

A Dell Book $3.50   (14367-5)

At your local bookstore or use this handy coupon for ordering:

| DELL BOOKS   IN JOY AND IN SORROW $3.50   (14367-5)
P.O. BOX 1000, PINE BROOK, N.J. 07058-1000

Please send me the books I have checked above. I am enclosing $ _____ (please add 75c per copy to cover postage and handling). Send check or money order—no cash or C.O.D.'s. Please allow up to 8 weeks for shipment.

Mr./Mrs./Miss _____

Address _____

City _____ State/Zip _____

The second volume in the
spectacular Heiress series

The Cornish Heiress

by Roberta Gellis
bestselling author of
The English Heiress

Meg Devoran—by night the flame-haired smuggler, Red Meg. Hunted and lusted after by many, she was loved by one man alone...

Philip St. Eyre—his hunger for adventure led him on a desperate mission into the heart of Napoleon's France.

From midnight trysts in secret smugglers' caves to wild abandon in enemy lands, they pursued their entwined destinies to the end—seizing ecstasy, unforgettable adventure—and love.

A Dell Book $3.50   (11515-9)

At your local bookstore or use this handy coupon for ordering:

| DELL BOOKS   THE CORNISH HEIRESS $3.50   (11515-9)
P.O. BOX 1000, PINE BROOK, N.J. 07058-1000

Please send me the books I have checked above. I am enclosing $ _____ (please add 75¢ per copy to cover postage and handling). Send check or money order—no cash or C.O.D.'s. Please allow up to 8 weeks for shipment.

Mr./Mrs./Miss _____

Address _____

City _____ State/Zip _____

Danielle Steel

AMERICA'S LEADING LADY OF ROMANCE REIGNS OVER ANOTHER BESTSELLER

A Perfect Stranger

A flawless mix of glamour and love by Danielle Steel, the bestselling author of *The Ring*, *Palomino* and *Loving*.

A DELL BOOK $3.50   #17221-7

At your local bookstore or use this handy coupon for ordering:

DELL BOOKS   A PERFECT STRANGER $3.50   #17221-7
P.O. BOX 1000, PINE BROOK, N.J. 07058-1000

Please send me the above title. I am enclosing $_____ (please add 75c per copy to cover postage and handling). Send check or money order—no cash or C.O.D.'s. Please allow up to 8 weeks for shipment.

Mr./Mrs./Miss _____

Address _____

City _____ State/Zip _____